Mindy

JUMANJI™

A Novelization by George Spelvin
Based on the Screenplay by Jonathan Hensleigh and Greg Taylor & Jim Strain
Based on a Screen Story by Greg Taylor & Jim Strain and Chris Van Allsburg
Based on the Book by Chris Van Allsburg

SCHOLASTIC INC.
New York   Toronto   London   Auckland   Sydney

ISBN 0-590-67909-0

12 11 10 9 8 7 6 5 4 3 2   5 6 7 8 9/9 0/0

Printed in the U.S.A   01

First Scholastic printing, December 1995

PROLOGUE

It is only a game.

Rules and a board. Tokens and dice. Pretty paintings.

An invitation to adventure. An escape from the mundane and into the savage unknown. All in the comfort of your own living room.

A game. No more, no less.

Until you play it.

For those few who have played, there has been no turning back.

And no one, not a single soul, has ever played it twice.

Welcome to Jumanji.

PART ONE

NEW HAMPSHIRE, 1869

CHAPTER 1

rrrraccck!
Lightning slashes the night sky, bathing the forest in a ghastly blue-white. For a moment, through the pelting rain, Caleb and Benjamin Sproul can see the steep walls of the hole they have dug.

The brothers hear a frightened, high-pitched whinny. In the nearby dirt road, their horse is pulling at its canvas-draped cart. Like any animal, like any sane human, it knows it should not be out in a night as brutal as this.

But even the horse's deep, primal fear cannot match the terror in the hearts of Caleb and Benjamin.

The terror caused by what is under the canvas.

Panting hard, eyes squinted against the rain,

the brothers throw their shovels out of the hole. They scramble upward.

Caleb runs to the cart. He lifts the canvas, revealing a padlocked iron box.

Benjamin stares at it, paralyzed.

"Come on!" Caleb shouts over the shrieking wind. "We're almost rid of it!"

The two boys drag the heavy box through the mud. At the hole, they lift it waist-high.

As they heave it over the edge, Benjamin's foot slips. Screaming, he tumbles in.

The box thumps to the bottom. Benjamin lands on top of it.

A drumming sound begins. Jungle drums, deep and pulsing, cutting through the storm's howl. The rhythm is fierce and warlike. But it is somehow sensuous and inviting. And completely irresistible.

Benjamin is frozen, his limbs locked with panic.

"No," Caleb whispers, his voice a rasp. "No!"

"It's after me!" The words explode from Benjamin. He leaps away from the box and tries to climb the muddy wall.

Caleb reaches down and pulls his brother to the surface. The drumming is louder now. Calling them both, summoning them back into the hole.

"Run!" Benjamin wails. "Run!"

Caleb grabs his brother by the shoulder. "No! We have to finish this! Help me bury it!"

They both pick up shovels. Grunting, at the brink of exhaustion, Caleb and Benjamin shovel clods of heavy, waterlogged soil into the hole.

Slowly the box is buried. The drumming grows fainter, then stops.

The boys turn back toward their horse, their chests heaving. They blink against the stinging rain.

"What if someone digs it up?" Benjamin shouts.

Caleb shakes his head solemnly as he throws his shovel into the cart. "May God have mercy on his soul."

Lightning splits the sky once more. Before the boom of thunder subsides, the boys are on the cart, driving their horse forward.

Caleb eyes a granite mile marker, carved with the words BRANTFORD — 1 MI.

In moments they will be home. Safe and dry.

Perhaps they will someday forget the awful box. Perhaps not. But at the very least, they have done their duty for future generations.

Under the ground, far from civilization, the box will harm no one.

As long as it stays there.

PART TWO

NEW HAMPSHIRE, 1969

CHAPTER 2

Nyeeaaaarrrr ... The B-52 bomber swoops down over the enemy encampment ... release bombs ... bank right and escape!

Alan Parrish took the sharp right turn onto Main Street. He was going at least fifteen miles an hour. Maybe twenty. These three-speed Schwinns were the best — speed, sturdiness, style. He darted up the driveway of the bakery, hopped the curb in front of the florist, shot into the street.

Prepare to strafe the supply crossroads ... now, while Field Marshal Harrison holds back the tank battalion!

At the corner of Elm and Main, Patrolman Harrison spotted Alan and held up traffic. "All yours, Alan!" he called out with a smile.

Alan bombed through. He glided into the town square and gave his usual quick nod toward a statue of his great-great-great-grandfather, the Civil War hero General Angus Parrish.

"Prepare to die, Parrish!" came a war cry from behind the statue.

Ambush!

It was Billy Jessup. Alan's worst nightmare. Half attack dog, half ape, wrapped up in the body of a thirteen-year-old boy. Dedicated to one major goal in life: destroying Alan Parrish.

For Billy, *strategy* usually meant saying "Come here" before throwing a punch. But he was getting smarter. He'd planned the ambush, and he'd brought along his entire gang of goons.

Alan pedaled furiously. Sweat tickled his brow. He could hear Billy's gang grunting behind him.

But Alan knew their weak spot. They owned Stingrays. Cool profile, teeny wheels. They had nothing on the Schwinn.

Alan turned off Main Street. He barreled up Mill Road. On one side of him, the Brantford River lapped peacefully past boulders and reeds. On the other, a small forest soon gave way to a wide, sunlit construction site.

And beyond that site was an old brick building that Alan knew almost as well as his house. His dad's shoe factory. Safety.

Alan's thighs screamed at him as he zoomed past the familiar sign:

PARRISH SHOES
FOUR GENERATIONS OF QUALITY

Dumping his bike near the front door, he scrambled inside.

Billy and his gang skidded to a stop. "Go ahead, run to Daddy!" Billy jeered. "We'll be waiting!"

Alan let the door shut behind him. He propped himself against the wall, gasping for breath.

Around him, the Parrish shoe factory buzzed with life. Craftspeople carefully cut and shaped what Alan's dad called "the shoes that keep New England walking." A conveyor belt carried leather soles toward an enormous stamping machine. Teams of workers stitched, dyed, buffed, and quality-tested, all on spanking clean tables and floors. The vaulted room was filled with raucous mechanical clanking.

Which, after what Alan had been through, was music to his ears.

Now, all he needed to do was keep in the shadows. Away from his dad. If *he* found out Alan was there —

"Hey, my man, Alan!"

Alan whirled around at the voice. Carl Bentley was waving at him, over by the sole-stamping machine.

Carl was cool. Of all the factory workers, he was among the youngest, boldest, and smartest. For 1969, most of the workers dressed pretty conservatively, but Carl wore bell-bottoms and had an Afro hairstyle. The younger workers called him the Sole Man.

"Hi, Carl," Alan greeted him.

"Let me show you something," Carl said. "I've been working on it for a year now, and I've got an appointment to show it to your dad this afternoon."

He held up the weirdest-looking shoe Alan had ever seen. It was made of canvas and leather, with racing stripes and padding — *lots* of padding. The sole was wide and thick, with a waffle pattern. Alan figured it was a sneaker of some kind, but it was nothing like the canvas Converses everyone wore. More like a sneaker from outer space.

"Well?" Carl grinned proudly. "Do you think he'll like it?"

12

"What is it?" Alan asked.

"What *is* it? It's the future. In a couple more years, there's going to be a pair of these in every closet in America. This shoe is going to be the height of fashion and — "

But Alan wasn't listening. Through a nearby window, he had caught a glimpse of Billy and his pals, wandering around. Waiting. Just as they'd promised.

"What's wrong?" Carl asked.

"Nothing," Alan shot back.

As Carl walked to the window to see for himself, a booming voice called out, "Alaaaan!"

Gulp.

Alan's heart sank so fast he had indigestion. Forcing a smile, he turned to face his dad.

Mr. Parrish walked the same way he ran his factory: headstrong, fast, and oblivious to anything in his way. A cloud of fragrant white smoke trailed from his ever-present pipe. His brows were knitted in an expression that looked, on the outside, like mild annoyance.

But Alan knew what was on the inside. And it was far from mild.

There were two things Alan's dad couldn't stand. Number one was idleness. Alan was not welcome in the factory unless he was learning or working.

Number two was weakness. To Mr. Parrish, running away was unmanly. A gentleman stood his ground, no matter what.

"What are you doing here?" Mr. Parrish asked sternly. "I've told you before, this factory isn't a playground."

Alan backed away. He dropped Carl's new-fangled shoe on the conveyor belt, which had stopped moving.

"I wanted to see if you could give me a ride home, Dad," Alan replied.

Mr. Parrish raised an eyebrow. "Billy Jessup again?"

Alan looked at the floor. Here it was again. The Lecture. This time, within earshot of Carl and all the shop managers.

"Son, you're going to have to deal with him sooner or later," Mr. Parrish intoned. "If you're afraid of something, you've got to face it."

The workers were pretending not to listen. Which meant they were hearing it all. Alan wanted to melt through the floor.

With a grim smile, Mr. Parrish patted Alan on the back. "Now get along, son."

Alan felt about two inches tall. He slunk away, staying close to the wall. The workers' pitying glances felt like tiny, intense heat lamps.

In his hurry to leave, he did not notice the conveyor belt starting up again.

Nor did he see Carl's futuristic athletic shoe trundling toward the stamping machine.

Neither did Carl. He was busy hearing his own, brief version of The Lecture.

"You know better than to let the boy play in here," Mr. Parrish said to him.

"Sorry, sir," Carl replied.

"Oh. I almost forgot. What was it you wanted to show me, Carl?"

Carl looked around for his shoe.

From the stamping machine came a loud shredding noise. Its slow rhythmic clank became frantic. The mechanism hacked and groaned, spitting bolts into the air among sparks and acrid smoke.

WAAAAW! WAAAAW! WAAAAW! WAAAAW!

The factory alarm sounded. Bewildered, Alan watched the entire place fall into chaos. His dad was barreling toward the machine, through a crowd of shouting, panicked workers.

Then, with a final shudder, the machine stopped.

Mr. Parrish pried open the smoking hulk.

He reached inside and pulled out a handful of charred, twisted canvas and leather strips.

Carl's face sank at the sight of his destroyed creation.

"Who did this?" Mr. Parrish demanded, glaring at Carl.

Hoo boy.

Alan did not want to stick around for the massacre. He turned tail and fled out the front door.

But he stopped short the moment he hit daylight. His brain was sending him a Jessup Alert.

Alan peered left and right. His bike was right where he'd left it, propped against the wall.

No Billy. No gang.

Hallelujah. They were probably off trying to steal shoelaces. Alan jumped on his bike. Mill Road yawned before him, open and free.

As he began to pedal, he spotted movement behind a tree on the left side of the road. Maybe a deer. He leaned instinctively the other way.

But it was not a deer. Or a bear. It was a bit higher on the food chain.

Just a bit.

Like a wolf pack, Billy and his pals sprang out from behind the trees.

And Alan was headed right for them.

CHAPTER 3

Screeech!

Alan jammed on his brake.

"Just because you're a Parrish," Billy snarled, "doesn't mean you can hang around with my girlfriend."

"You mean *Sarah?*" Alan couldn't believe what he was hearing. Was that why they were chasing him? Sarah Whittle was a neighbor — kind of a loudmouth, but a decent snowball target in winter and an okay person. That was it.

"But we've always been friends," Alan explained.

Billy grinned. "Not anymore."

His goons roared with laughter, as if Billy's joke were some kind of high wit. Then, with carnivorous smiles, they approached Alan.

He stood, lock-kneed, mulling over his choices: In front of him was certain doom. Behind him, his dad's lecture series. Running would be useless and standing still would be stupid.

Stupidity won. The boys leaped all over him. Alan tried to fight back, but that only made things worse.

He felt lucky his head stayed on his shoulders. The jolts to his stomach were so strong he thought their fists would go right through him.

When they tossed him in a ditch, bruised and bloody, he felt like a chewed-up, spat-out piece of Bazooka.

Groaning and swollen, he dragged himself out of the ditch. In the distance he could see his tormentors speeding away on their Stingrays.

Except for Billy. He was now riding Alan's Schwinn, zigzagging down the road, laughing.

Alan spat blood. "Jerks," he muttered.

As he struggled to his feet, he glanced nervously at the factory windows. As bad as he felt, one thing could make him feel worse. Only one thing was more humiliating than being beat up by Billy Jessup.

Being beat up in front of his dad.

A grid of dull gray windows stared back at him. No angry, glaring, disappointed face in any of them. With a slight sense of relief, Alan turned away and began hobbling home. His shirt was a filthy, tattered rag, his legs stiff and bruised.

Great. How on earth was he going to hide *this* from his parents? He could see the future laid out ahead of him. His mom in tears, calling the Jessups to complain. Retaliation from Billy. More calls. More retaliation. Nightly sermons from Dad. Boxing lessons. Wilderness survival trips. Leadership training camps.

And then, years from now, for good measure, Dad would force Alan into the shoe business and hire Billy as his boss.

A lifetime of absolute misery.

Tears filled the slits of Alan's swelling eyelids. I hate *hate* HATE this life! he thought. If only he could escape Brantford and its stupid kids and the rotten, totally oppressive Parrish family dynasty. If only his Schwinn really were a fighter plane and could take him far, far away . . . .

A drumming sound interrupted his thoughts.

Terrific. A migraine headache. Maybe a broken eardrum, or a concussion. Nothing like adding a little injury to the insult.

He shook his head. He inserted a finger into his ear and wiggled it hard.

The sound was still there. Louder.

No, this couldn't be a headache. It wasn't the regular throb of a heartbeat. It was a strange rhythm, wild and primitive, almost warlike.

But the weird thing was, it filled Alan with a funny kind of joy. Half of him wanted to run away, but the other half wanted to dance.

The sound was coming from across the street. From the construction site just beyond the ancient mile marker, the one that said BRANTFORD — 1 MI in worn-out letters under decades of moss.

Alan stepped closer. The beat quickened. It was as if the drummers knew he was approaching. As if they were beckoning him.

He walked to the edge of the site. Standing near a sign that said FUTURE EXECUTIVE OFFICES OF PARRISH SHOES, he peered over the edge of a huge pit. He had seen the plans for the new building. Someday it would double the size of the factory.

But right now it was a humongous hole in the ground. Filled with trucks, machinery, workers, equipment . . . and the coolest drumbeat he'd ever heard.

He scanned the area. On the other side of the pit, a snack truck was driving down a ramp.

Most of the workers had dropped their tools and were heading for it.

The drums were furious now, deafening. But nowhere could Alan see a band. And not one of the workers seemed to notice the sound at all.

It's just for me.

The thought popped into his head.

Alan smiled. He was hearing things. He had a screw loose. That had to be it.

He turned to leave.

Now the drums seemed to be shaking the earth. As if an army of jungle warriors were about to erupt from the ground.

From the ground.

Under the ground.

That was where the drums were. Alan didn't know how he knew that. But he did.

Slowly he scanned the open pit, looking for a pathway down.

What am I doing?

Climbing in was a ridiculous idea. In his condition, he was liable to fall and break his neck.

But hey, if you didn't give it a try, you'd never know.

Taking a deep breath, Alan carefully lowered himself into the pit.

21

When he reached the bottom, he realized the pain was gone.

The bruises and cuts were there, but he barely felt them. The drumbeat seemed to have entered his body, washing through it, giving him strength. Alan felt electrically charged. Every pore tingled with a sense of adventure.

He followed the frenzied sound, stumbling through a maze of tall concrete forms.

Just beyond them, he stopped.

The wall.

The dirt wall of the pit. That was where the drums were buried.

The soil was packed pretty hard, but Alan dug his hands into it. He scraped clods of dirt, pulled out tiny roots, sent an earthworm flying.

Less than a foot in, his fingertips hit something solid. Some sort of handle, metal and corroded.

He grabbed hold, planted his feet, and pulled.

The box dislodged. Alan jerked backward and fell to the ground. Dirt showered around him.

Instantly the drums stopped.

In Alan's lap was a rusted, padlocked metal box. Alan set it on the ground and grabbed a nearby shovel. He lifted it high and brought it down directly on the lock.

With a dull clack, it broke in two and fell off.

Slowly Alan lifted the top.

CHAPTER 4

S and.

The box was filled with sand.

I really am going crazy, Alan thought. With a sigh, he stood up and walked away.

There it was again. The drumming. Loud and furious, practically boxing his ears.

Alan spun around, kneeled, and dug his hands into the box. Under the sand, his fingers touched something solid.

He pulled upward. As the sand fell away, Alan saw he was holding a rectangular wooden box. Hinges lined one of the long sides, and on the other was a clasp. Like a wooden chess or backgammon board.

The wood was shiny and smooth. Under the clear lacquer was a painting so rich and glorious it could have been made yesterday. Among vivid deep green jungle vines and distant amber savannahs were lions, monkeys, exotic birds, and stampeding rhinos. A broad-shouldered, mustached hunter stood in the center of it all, wearing a pith helmet and clutching a rifle.

Across the top, in brilliant, fancy letters, was a strange word.

Jumanji.

Alan shook the box. Something inside rattled.

Carefully he unhooked the clasp and pried open the two halves of the board.

From within the box, he caught a flash of bright color. But before he could examine it, he heard voices behind him. Workers were approaching.

The last thing he needed was for the men to report him to his dad.

Snapping the box shut, Alan climbed out of the hole.

The walk home was long and torturous. Alan's cuts had begun to sting, his lip and eyes to throb with pain.

The Parrish house stood at the highest point of Brantford, way up on Jefferson Street. It was the largest and oldest house in town, a mansion built by General Angus Parrish with the spoils of the Civil War. No expense had been spared by the general — carved oak doors, a grand entry foyer and vaulted living room, a fireplace large enough to roast a side of beef, an antique grandfather clock the size of a small tree, enough bedrooms for a large family and servants, and a tremendous attic.

Alan's family didn't have the servants and the grand lifestyle, but they had kept the house lovingly. It was in tip-top shape, a regular stop on several New Hampshire historical country tours.

But Alan was thinking about none of that as he sneaked in the front door. His number-one concern was silence. If his mom saw him, she'd freak. And he was dying to open the box.

He tiptoed across the living room floor, sat on the sofa, and flipped open the latch.

"Wowww . . ." he murmured.

It was a board game, all right, but not like any he'd ever seen before. The board was solid, hand-carved wood. Four pathways of blank squares wound through a bright, riotous painting — jungle animals and lush trees, stylized like an old circus poster. At the center of it all was a glassy circle of deep black. Off to the side, a compartment held a pair of dice and four small playing tokens.

Alan held up one of the tokens, an intricately carved African statuette.

"Alan?" his mom's voice called out. "Are you home?"

Yikes. Alan put the token down on the board, glancing anxiously toward the living room door.

Had he been looking down, he would have seen the token slide, quickly, silently across the board.

When it reached the first square of one of the paths, it stopped.

Ready to begin play.

But Alan didn't see a thing. He slammed the board shut and shoved it under the sofa as his mom appeared in the doorway.

When she saw his condition, her smile immediately fell.

"Oh, Alan," she groaned, "not *again*."

Alan explained everything to his mom, except the Jumanji box. Later for that.

After showering and dressing, he felt a little better. But not much.

Alan had one consolation for the miserable day. His mom and dad were going out that night to some fancy, black-tie party.

Which meant dinner alone. And no long, excruciating Lecture.

Cleaned up and dressed in intact clothes,

Alan picked at his meal. The Parrish dinner table loomed before him, thick, dark, and highly polished. It seemed, to him, the size of a football field. Probably an antique from the days when the entire king's court ate together. You could pass a hot platter of mashed potatoes and it would be cold by the time it reached the other end.

Clunk, clunk, clunk . . . Alan heard his dad's unmistakable footsteps coming down the stairs of the front foyer. And then his voice: "Hard work, determination, and a cheerful outlook . . ."

Ugh. Leave it to Dad. A sermon at all costs.

" . . . Attributes that have exemplified the Brantford spirit since our forefathers first settled this town," Mr. Parrish continued, still in the foyer. "Despite the granite of our soil and the harshness of our native clime, we have . . . we have . . . *what?*"

"Prospered?" came Mrs. Parrish's voice. "Persisted?"

"I knew the whole speech by heart this morning!"

Alan sighed with relief. A speech. Good. Let other people squirm.

For a moment, his mom and dad muttered softly to one another. Then they walked into the dining room. "Well," said Mr. Parrish stiffly, "we're on our way."

"Okay," Alan replied with a shrug.

"Alan," his mom interjected, "I told your father what you told me this afternoon. That it wasn't just Billy Jessup."

She gave Mr. Parrish a look, and he shuffled awkwardly. "If I'd known that," he said, "I wouldn't have . . ."

Typical Dad. When he wanted action he could find the words, but he was like a stumbling little kid when it came to admitting he was wrong.

"It's okay, Dad," Alan said.

"But I wanted you to know how proud I am of you," Mr. Parrish went on. "You faced them even though you were outnumbered. And since you took it like a man . . ." He pulled a brochure out of his pocket and laid it in front of Alan. "Your mother and I have decided that you're ready to go to the Cliffside Academy for Boys. You proved it today."

"Congratulations, sweetheart," Mrs. Parrish said, leaning down to kiss Alan.

Alan gaped at the brochure. It showed a well-scrubbed, dorky-looking guy in a jacket and tie. Walking cheerfully past an ivy-covered building, he held a stack of books that would give a gorilla a hernia.

This was a boarding school, Alan remembered. They wanted to send him away.

"You don't want me living here anymore," Alan said.

"Oh, Alan, how could you possibly think such a thing?" Mrs. Parrish exclaimed.

"You're ashamed of me getting beat up all the time," Alan went on.

"I just told you how proud I am of you, son," his dad retorted. "And it's always been the plan that you'd go to Cliffside when you were ready. I mean, Parrishes have been going there since the seventeen-hundreds."

Alan looked closely at the photo. "Look at this — 'Parrish Hall'! The kids are always on my case because I'm a Parrish. Wait till I'm living in a building named after me!"

Mr. Parrish looked insulted. "It's the main dormitory. It was named after my father!"

"Good," Alan replied. "Why don't you live in it?"

"I did. And I wouldn't be who I am today if it weren't for my years there. So don't get smart with me, Alan — "

"I'm not! Maybe I don't want to be who you are! Maybe I don't even want to be a Parrish!"

"Believe me, you won't be!" Now his dad's face was turning red with fury. Mrs. Parrish put a gentle hand on his shoulder but it did no good. "Not until you start acting like one!"

With that, Mr. Parrish stalked toward the door.

"So I guess I'm not ready to go to Cliffside, then," Alan murmured.

Mr. Parrish wheeled around. "We're taking you there next Sunday, and I don't want to hear another word about it!"

"You won't!" Alan shot back, fighting tears. "I'm never going to talk to you again!"

For a moment, Alan's dad just stared at him, a mixture of shock and disgust on his face. Then, wordlessly, he signaled to Mrs. Parrish, and they both walked out of the house.

Alan's eyes filled with tears. Hurt and anger and exhaustion roiled around inside of him like a pack of fighting animals.

He ripped the brochure to shreds, letting the pieces fall to the table. If they wanted him to leave home, fine. He'd do it right now and get it over with. And it wouldn't be to Cliffside Academy.

He would run away forever.

CHAPTER 5

Alan ran up to his bedroom. He flung open his closet and grabbed a suitcase. Only the necessities, he told himself. He dumped in some clothes and supplies, then clomped down to the kitchen and swiped a jar of peanut butter and a box of cookies.

Halfway across the front foyer, Alan remembered the box. He darted back into the living room, pulled it from under the sofa, and stuffed it into the suitcase. Then he sprinted to the front door.

Ding-dong!

The sound of the bell made Alan jump. Quickly he shoved his suitcase under a nearby table and pulled open the door.

Standing on the stoop, smiling, was Sarah Whittle. The source of Alan's pain and suffering.

32

The Official Girlfriend of the Eighth-Grader from the Black Lagoon, Billy Jessup.

"Oh," Alan said flatly, grabbing the suitcase. "It's you."

"Are you going somewhere?" Sarah asked.

"Yeah, I'm — " Alan caught a glimpse of his Schwinn on the sidewalk behind Sarah. "I was just going to Billy's to get that bike."

"With your suitcase?"

Alan brushed past her silently and began strapping his suitcase to his bike rack.

"I told Billy if he didn't give your bike back, I wouldn't go to the movies with him this weekend," Sarah said.

"Great," Alan replied drily. "Thanks a lot."

"Hey, I just wanted him to stop picking on you. I was trying to do you a favor."

Alan began wheeling his bike away from the house. "Save it for your boyfriend."

"Billy's *not* my boyfriend!" Sarah retorted. "But at least he's my own age."

"Yeah, but mentally I could be his grandfather. And I'm only ten months younger than you."

Sarah glared at him. "But you're so immature!"

"Fine," Alan called over his shoulder. "Have a great life with Billy."

Boom-b-b-boom-b-b-boom . . .

The drumbeat blasted for a moment, then ended. Alan stopped in his tracks.

"What was that?" Sarah called out.

"Nothing," Alan answered.

As he started walking, the drums sounded again.

"What's *in* there?" Sarah asked.

Alan looked at the dark road. By now he should be speeding away. Escaping Brantford. Spending the night in some . . . what? Five-dollar-a-night motel? No such thing, but five dollars was all he had. Camping on the side of the road, with mosquitoes and raccoons and slugs? Uh-uh.

And what was going to happen if he tried to play Jumanji alone? What if the game needed two or more players?

Sarah was staring at the suitcase. She could hear the drums. She'd want to play. And even Sarah was better than nobody.

Alan wheeled his bike around. "You have to see this," he said. "It's really cool."

They both raced back to the house.

Inside, Alan took out the game and unfolded it on the floor. Sarah picked up the dice and examined them. Alan searched for instructions.

Neither had noticed the token standing on the first square, unbudged from where it had slid earlier.

"It's so weird. I mean, where does the drumming come from?" Alan read aloud the instructions printed on the cover: " 'Jumanji, a game for those who seek to find a way to leave the world behind. The first to get to the end of the path and yell "Jumanji" wins.' "

Sarah made a face. "I quit playing board games five years ago."

She casually dropped the dice on the board. They turned up a four and a two.

The token began to move. It slid exactly six spaces forward.

This time, Alan and Sarah were watching.

Their jaws practically hit the floor.

CHAPTER 6

"It's got to be magnetized or something," Alan guessed. Sarah did not answer. Her eyes were fixed on the glassy black circle in the center of the board.

"Alan, look!" she exclaimed.

In a smoky swirl, a message took form:

At night they fly; you'd better run!

These winged things are not much fun.

Alan picked up the dice and read the words aloud. As the letters faded, a flapping noise came from the chimney.

Sarah sat up with a start. "What was that?"

"I don't know," Alan replied.

"Put the game away, Alan." Sarah's voice was trembling.

GONNNNG! GONNNNG! GONNNNG!

The grandfather clock shocked Alan out of his seat. His hair stood on end. His dice went flying.

They clattered to the board: two and three.

Another token slid out of the compartment, onto one of the other paths, and moved ahead five spaces.

"Oh, no!" Alan gasped as another message appeared:

In the jungle you must wait,
Until the dice read five or eight.

"In the jungle you must wait?" Alan repeated. "What's *that* mean?"

"*Alan, what's happening to you?*"

Sarah's shriek took Alan by surprise. She was gawking at him as if he'd grown fangs.

"What do you mean?" he asked. "Nothing's happening to — "

A wispy, vaporous tendril flicked Alan's nose. He glanced down and saw that smoke was rising from the black circle, twining around his body, quickly enveloping him in a thick gray twister.

"What — " he stammered. "What — "

Then, before he could move a muscle, he felt his body lurching downward.

He let out a piercing scream. It echoed wildly, caroming off the walls of the living room.

And it only stopped when Alan was sucked into the game board.

Sarah sat, locked in place. Her muscles couldn't move. The blood rushed from her face.

He was gone. Into the game.

Into a game?

In the black circle was now a miniature world, a dense jungle with swaying fronds and a twisty river.

From within it, Alan's voice blared out, "Sarah? *Saraaaaah!*"

"Alan?" Sarah whispered in horror.

Slowly the jungle scene faded to black.

And Sarah once again noticed the flapping noise.

It was tremendous now. Like a miniature thunderstorm inside the chimney.

In a sudden explosion, hundreds of bats poured into the room. They filled the air, screeching, lunging, dive-bombing.

"YEEEEEEEEEAGGGHH!" Sarah ran into the front foyer, followed by a writhing cloud of black. The bats surrounded her, smacking against her, pulling her hair.

She fell to her knees. Crawling blindly, she made it to the front door.

Sarah struggled to her feet and pushed the door open. The bats flew into the night air.

Beneath them, Sarah ran and ran.

People in Brantford later said that Sarah's

screams could be heard all the way to Main Street. That she ran so far and so fast, the police had to pick her up in the next town.

Whether those things were true or not, two things were certain. Alan was gone. And Sarah refused to go near the Parrish house ever again.

PART THREE

NEW HAMPSHIRE, 1995

CHAPTER 7

J udy and Peter Shepherd hated the house.

Sure it was big. And their aunt Nora, who was dying to buy it, kept calling it "so old," as if that were a compliment. It was built by a Civil War general, she said.

Well, since when did generals know how to build good houses? And besides, they didn't have electricity in the Civil War days. Or Jacuzzis. Or microwaves. Or anything remotely cool that belonged in a house. Even Peter knew that, and he was only eight.

Aunt Nora's heels clicked crisply on the cracked front walkway. Next to her, the real-estate woman, Ms. Winston, couldn't stop chattering.

"I'm glad you decided to buy this place," she chirped. "I think a bed-and-breakfast is just what this town needs."

"Well, it was hard to turn it down at this price," Aunt Nora replied. "Especially full of furniture."

Ms. Winston opened the front door, and they all stepped into the house's front foyer.

"Boy . . ." Aunt Nora said with a gasp. "I keep forgetting how big this place is."

Gross, Judy thought. That was the word Aunt Nora meant. A synonym for big. Also the perfect word to describe the inside of the old Parrish mansion.

Cobwebs stretched across the ceiling, so ragged and thick with dust that it looked as if miniature spider laundry hung from them. The living room was so enormous you could play baseball inside it. The fireplace bricks were mossy and the hearth was covered with some green, funky-looking grunge. Mounted on the wall above it was a long saber in a glass case. The furniture, if that's what it was, lay hidden under sheets gray with age. A grandfather clock stood against the wall, broken and sad-looking, sort of like a corpse.

Judy and Peter exchanged a look. This was not the future they'd had in mind . . . .

"I'm going to put a reception area right here," Aunt Nora declared, gesturing toward the front of the foyer, "and a bar over here in the parlor. . . . "

"Sounds lovely," Ms. Winston piped up. "I'm sure you and your kids are going to be very happy here."

Aunt Nora leaned closely in to Ms. Winston and murmured, "Actually, they're my late brother's kids. He and his wife passed away four months ago."

Ugh. Did Aunt Nora really think they couldn't hear her? Judy wondered. Was she trying to spare their feelings or something?

Fat chance. Since their parents' deaths, Judy and Peter couldn't possibly have felt more rotten. Mom and Dad were supposed to have been gone only a week. A skiing trip in the Canadian Rockies. They'd called it their second honeymoon. Judy's biggest worry was that Dad might break his leg on the slope. But a fatal car wreck? No kid was ever prepared to hear that.

Not to mention what came afterward. The pitying stares, the soft, oversensitive way people thought they had to speak to you. The phone calls and family battles over custody. And the questions! It was always the same ones, over and over.

Poor Peter. He'd just clammed right up. Hadn't said a word to anyone but Judy since the accident. As for Judy, well, she went the other direction — why say nothing when you could ... *embellish* a little? It was more fun to make up explanations. Describe things the way you wanted them to be. Watch whether people believed you or not. Usually they did.

Aunt Nora believed they needed a "fresh start." And she was an antique freak who'd always wanted to run an inn. So here they were, plucked out of their hometown, away from their old friends. In run-down Brantford, New Hampshire, on a spring Sunday before a school day.

What a comfort.

Ms. Winston smiled at Peter. "So what do you think, young man? Is it big enough for you?"

Peter turned silently and walked out of the room.

"He hasn't spoken a word since it happened," Judy explained.

"Oh, my." Ms. Winston's lips curled down into an expression Judy knew well. The *boy-I'm-uncomfortable-but-I'll-appear-sympathetic* look. "I'm sorry. How terribly awful."

"It's okay," Judy lied. "We barely knew our parents. They were always away, skiing in St.

Moritz, gambling in Monte Carlo, safariing in darkest Africa. We didn't know if they even loved us. But when the sheik's yacht went down, they managed to write us a really beautiful good-bye note which was found floating in a champagne bottle among the debris."

With a shrug, she walked away. Leaving Ms. Winston in a daze.

As Judy headed down the hall toward the stairway, she heard Aunt Nora whispering, "They were very devoted parents. It was a car wreck in Canada."

Sigh. Foiled again.

Judy passed by an archway to a grand library. Dark-wood bookcases stretched from floor to ceiling, stuffed with dusty leather-bound books. Off to one side was a glass-enclosed sunroom, glowing dimly with the daylight reflected through window grime.

Peter was in there. Judy watched him pull an old sheet off a bronze bust. She could hear him gasp as the stern eyes of General Angus Parrish glared at him.

Some cheerful house.

For a single woman, Aunt Nora sure had a lot of junk. That afternoon, after unloading the moving van, the whole huge mansion seemed stuffed with her boxes.

It was going to take them forever to unpack.

The bedrooms were all off a long corridor on the second floor. As Peter and Judy lugged their suitcases toward their rooms, they spotted Aunt Nora struggling with a door at the end of the hall. With an exasperated sigh, she said, "Have to get a locksmith for this one."

Peter scampered to the door and peeked through the keyhole. All he could see was a picture frame on the wall and a trophy on a dresser. A kid's room. Maybe there was some cool stuff inside, he thought.

"Okay, you kids," Aunt Nora called out, "let's get this all cleaned up. Peter, take that suitcase up to the attic. Then we can all have ice cream."

As Judy continued to her room, Peter grabbed a flashlight from a cardboard box, then dragged his aunt's suitcase up the attic stairs. At the top was a wooden door, slightly open.

He pushed it with his shoulder. Slowly it swung inward.

EEEEEEEEEEE . . .

The creak echoed into the pitch-black space. A blast of cold, clammy air rushed out.

And then a slight noise. A flapping sound.
Go away!

Peter ignored the voice in his head. The room was scary, but it was the coolest thing he'd seen in the house.

He flicked on his flashlight and leaned in.

Two dark eyes glared back at him.

Peter jumped back. Hiding behind the doorjamb, he peered in again. The eyes belonged to a face in a painting, a stuffy old dude who looked related to the bust of General Angus Parrish.

He swung the light from right to left. Like the rest of the house, the room was crammed full. Old steamer trunks against the wall. Furniture sagging under the weight of cardboard boxes. An upright piano. Above it all were wooden rafters studded with nails, from which hung all kinds of junk — coats, blankets, camping and sports equipment. . . .

And some black, shriveled, leathery thing.

Peter stepped in a little closer. Was it some kind of old-fashioned baseball mitt?

Nope.

Baseball mitts didn't move.

They also did not fly.

Or screech.

Or attack eight-year-old kids.

"YEEEEEEEAAGGGHHH!" Peter dropped his flashlight and ran.

A giant bat was swooping toward him, flashing its razor-sharp teeth!

CHAPTER 8

J udy and Aunt Nora rushed to the bottom of the attic stairs.

Peter burst out the door. He slammed it shut behind him. Stumbling down the steps, he nearly knocked Aunt Nora off her feet.

"What?" she demanded.

Thud.

They all shot a glance upstairs.

The sound was loud. Heavy. Muffled.

"I'm going to Motel Six," Judy vowed.

Aunt Nora gave them both a dismissive look. "Oh, for heaven's sake . . ."

As she stomped bravely upstairs, Judy and Peter huddled behind her. Grabbing the door-knob, Aunt Nora pushed the door open.

THUMP!

That sound was even louder than the other. And closer.

Aunt Nora yanked the door shut and hurried away. "Maybe I'll get somebody over here to take a look in the morning."

That night, Judy heard another noise. She was lying in her new room, trying to fall asleep.

The sound was in the attic. But it wasn't a dull thud. It didn't sound as if a creature was up there anymore.

It sounded like drums.

No way was she going to be alone tonight. Judy crept out of bed. As she ran down the hall to Peter's room, the drums faded.

Peter was awake, too. Looking at a photo of their mom and dad. Which he stuffed into a night table drawer as soon as Judy burst in.

"Move over," she demanded, sliding under the covers with him. "Did you hear anything a little while ago?"

Peter wrinkled his brow.

"Me neither," Judy quickly interjected.

They both fell silent, listening to the sound of crickets and a passing car.

"I miss Mom and Dad," Peter finally said. "Do you?"

"No," Judy replied softly.

"Liar. If you don't cut it out, you're going to get sent to a shrink."

"Where do you think they're going to send you if you don't start talking?"

With a scowl, Peter turned away.

Judy felt awful. She knew she'd been too hard on Peter. At a time like this, he was all she had in the world.

She nestled her face in the pillow and hugged her brother. Slowly her eyes began to close.

And the drums began again.

Her eyes sprang open. Something was up there. Something very, very weird.

Unless it was her imagination. Post-traumatic shock, or whatever they called that.

She debated waking up Peter but decided not to.

The exterminator was coming tomorrow. Maybe he'd find an old tape recorder up there. Or a family of musical bats. If not, Judy was going to plan drastic measures.

A foster family in Siberia might be nice.

Judy didn't know how she managed to sleep at all. But she and Peter must have managed, because when the doorbell rang the next morning, it awakened them.

It was the exterminator, right on time. As Aunt Nora escorted him into the attic, Judy and Peter quickly ate breakfast and washed up. To show the man what the bat looked like, Peter found the "Bats of the World" entry in his encyclopedia.

Then he and Judy ran upstairs and awaited the exterminator's verdict outside the attic door.

After poking around awhile, the man emerged with a friendly shrug. "I don't see any guano."

Peter held out the open encyclopedia and pointed to a photo.

The exterminator chuckled. "That's an *African* bat, son. We don't get bats like that in New England."

"But that's what he saw," Judy insisted.

"Well, whatever it was is gone now," the exterminator replied. "Bats aren't what I'd worry about in this house, anyways."

The comment hung in the air like a foul smell. "What *would* you worry about?" Judy asked.

"Well, personally, I wouldn't want to live in a house where someone was murdered."

Judy and Peter shot each other a glance. "*Murdered?*" Judy repeated.

"Yup. Little Alan Parrish. He just vanished, about twenty-five years ago. Some say it was kidnap, but nobody ever came around asking for money. I say his father did it. It's a shame, too, because the Parrishes used to be quite a family around here. But he was having trouble with the kid, and one day he just lost it. You can bet if it hadn't been a Parrish, the cops would have torn this place apart looking for the remains — but seeing how the family practically owned the town, they got special treatment." The exterminator ducked into the attic and gazed around, squint-eyed. "There's a thousand and one places he could have hid the body in this house, especially if he chopped it up first."

Judy felt her breakfast churning around in her stomach. Boy, how many cheery things this house had going for it.

"Hey, up there!" Aunt Nora called up from the second floor. "You don't want to be late for your first day of school!"

"Not a bat in sight, ma'am," the exterminator announced.

Aunt Nora smiled. "See, kids? There's nothing in the house to be afraid of."

Right, Judy thought.

Body parts in the walls. Thumping in the attic. Disappearing giant bats. Jungle drums.

Nothing to be afraid of at all.

CHAPTER 9

E yes. That was Judy's first impression of her sixth-grade homeroom at Brantford Junior High. Dozens of eyes, staring at her. Sizing her up. Wanting to know everything about her.

Although it was a cool day, Judy's sweaty shirt collar stuck to her neck.

Her teacher, Ms. Kiely, was smiling at her as if she were a cute stray puppy who'd just wandered in. "Class," Ms. Kiely announced, "we have a new member this year, all the way from Philadelphia. Judy, why don't you stand up and tell us a little about yourself?"

Judy took a deep breath. The eyes were burning into her now. Her heart felt like a washing machine in mid-cycle.

"Ummmm, my name is Judy Shepherd, and my brother and I just moved to Brantford to stay with our aunt, because . . ." *Go for it*, her brain commanded her. *Make it good!* "Because my parents were abducted by Maoist guerrillas in Papua New Guinea, where they were researching these strange new rain-forest viruses. They were warned not to go in because the political situation was so unstable, but they felt that in the name of science, it was their duty. . . ."

Ms. Kiely's smile faded. But Judy had only begun.

By recess, she'd added several new chapters to the story. And she managed to attract a huge playground audience — including Peter.

". . . So because of the top-secret nature of their work," she explained, wrapping up her story, "the rescue mission was called off until the State Department figures out a way to keep the whole thing quiet."

She beamed at her listeners. In the back of the crowd, Peter stared solemnly at the ground.

"If they were so concerned about keeping it quiet," a girl called out, "why'd they tell *you*?"

"She's lying!" shouted a smirking, heavyset boy. "My mom sold them their house and told me all about it. Her parents aren't ~~~ They're *dead!*"

Peter looked up, his face crimson. He leaped at the boy, fists flying.

"Peter, don't!" Judy yelled.

Too late. Peter sank his teeth into his tormentor's arm.

"Yeeeeaaaahhhhhh!" the boy screamed. "He *bit* me!"

As he ran away, crying, Peter bared his teeth and snarled at the other kids.

"He bites!" one girl taunted.

"He thinks he's an animal!" shouted another.

Judy had had enough. She grabbed her brother by the arm and pulled him away.

As they headed back into the school, the catcalls and jeers echoed through the playground.

That night, at the dinner table, Aunt Nora was furious. "I can't believe I have to talk to the principal after your first *day!* What am I supposed to do with you? This is *not* my department."

"You'd better punish us," Judy suggested. "You should probably ground us."

"Yeah?" Aunt Nora furrowed her brows anx-

_...., you're both grounded! Now, ... and relax, finish our dinner, and ... something else."

...y silently ate.

"Well," Judy finally piped up, "we found out why you got the house so cheap. Twenty-five years ago, a kid named Alan Parrish used to live here. Then one day he disappeared. The police searched everywhere, but they never found him because his parents chopped him up in little pieces and hid them in the walls. Everybody in town thinks the place is haunted."

Aunt Nora's fork clattered to the plate. "That's _it_! I am sick and tired of your lies, young lady. You're grounded!"

"You already did that one," Judy reminded her. She waited to hear her next punishment, but Aunt Nora just stared at her, sputtering. So Judy offered, "Send me to my room."

Wearily, Aunt Nora nodded.

Judy stood up and walked away. As she passed through the dining room door, she said, "But just for your information, that _wasn't_ a lie."

The next morning, Judy and Peter waited glumly in the front hall for the school bus. Aunt

Nora bustled downstairs, dressed for a day of business meetings.

"There's a snack for you in the fridge for when you get home," she said. "If I get held up at the permit office, I'll call."

Boom-b-b-boom . . . boom-b-b-boom . . .

Judy spun around toward the sound upstairs.

She noticed that Peter had, too. Had he heard? Or was he just reacting to her?

"Are you listening to me?" Aunt Nora asked. "Hello? Hmm, maybe I should wait with you till the bus comes. Did your parents used to put you on the bus?"

"No," Judy said.

"Are you sure? You seem distracted."

Didn't she hear? Judy couldn't believe it. The drums were pounding away, and Aunt Nora seemed oblivious.

Judy ran to the front door and held it open. "Don't worry, we'll be fine."

Aunt Nora gave her a dubious look. "All right . . . be good." Checking her watch, she walked out to her car.

Judy quickly shut the door. The drumming halted.

"You *do* hear it!" Judy said to Peter.

"Hear what?" Peter asked.

BOOM-B-B-BOOM . . . BOOM-B-B-BOOM . . .

He heard that, all right. His hair was standing on end.

Tripping over their feet, they both raced upstairs.

Then, as they reached the bottom of the attic steps, the drums fell silent.

Judy swallowed. Peter's breaths were shallow, rapid, and jarringly loud in the quiet.

The attic door stood slightly ajar. Slowly, side by side, Judy and Peter crept up the stairs.

Judy pushed the door open. Morning sun filtered through the tiny windows, casting the abandoned junk in a sickly, shadowy gray.

"Where was it coming from?" Judy asked, as she walked slowly into the room.

Peter shook his head, walking the other way.

The floorboards creaked under their weight.

BOOM-BOOOOOOM-B-B-B-BOOM-BOOM-BOOOM!

Judy shrieked so loud her throat hurt.

She had her answer. It was right behind her — in a pile of old toys and games!

Peter ran to it. He and Judy began digging toward the sound, throwing aside boxes, baseball gloves, tennis rackets. The farther they dug, the louder was the drumming.

When they reached the bottom, the noise was unbearable.

And only one box was left.

A beautiful wooden box that said *Jumanji*.

CHAPTER 10

"**W**ow . . ." Judy whispered.

The drumming had stopped again, and Peter had unfolded the game board atop an old dresser. He and Judy stood in silent awe. The painting, the jet-black circle, the delicate carving — it was all so lifelike.

Two black tokens stood on the board — on the sixth square of one path, and the fifth of another. Peter tried to pick them up.

"Weird," he said. "They're stuck."

He pulled the dice and the other two tokens out of the side compartment. As he examined them, Judy read the instructions: " 'Jumanji, a game for those who seek to find a way to leave the world behind.' "

The two tokens flew out of Peter's hand. They landed on the first squares of the remaining unoccupied paths.

Peter shot his sister a look of utter panic.

"It's got to be . . . microchips or something," Judy said.

She took the dice from his hands and looked them over.

"You go first," Peter insisted.

Judy gulped. "Okay."

She let the dice drop to the board.

Six and three. Nine.

The drumming started again. One of the two unplayed tokens moved ahead nine spaces.

Judy and Peter watched, frozen with amazement, as a message formed in the black circle:

A tiny bite can make you itch,
Make you sneeze, make you twitch.

As the letters faded, a buzzing noise began above their heads.

Three mosquitoes were flying toward them. Mosquitoes the size of pigeons. With stingers like knives.

Judy grabbed a tennis racket and swung. With a sharp *smack*, she sent one of the mosquitoes crashing through a window.

The other two flew after it, escaping outside.

Peter picked up the dice and looked at them curiously. Then he began to roll.

"*Don't!*" Judy warned him.

Too late.

Snake eyes. One and one.

The last token shifted ahead two spaces. And another message appeared in the center:

This will not be an easy mission;

Monkeys slow the expedition.

A loud crash rang out from downstairs.

"What's that?" Judy asked.

She and Peter ran out the door. As they sped down the attic steps, they heard another crash.

From the kitchen.

They bolted to the first floor. The banging and smashing were out of control, and now they could hear wild screeching.

Judy pushed open the kitchen door.

Monkeys?

The place was teeming with them. At least a dozen. One was pitching porcelain cups to another, who smashed them with a soup ladle. Others were raiding the refrigerator, throwing food, spilling milk.

Thwack!

A carving knife lodged in the doorjamb. Peter jumped back. Across the kitchen, a leering monkey reared back to try again, this time with a meat cleaver.

Time to go. Judy and Peter raced back up to the attic. They dived at the board.

lion bellowed. With a loud *crrraaaaack*, five sharp claws smashed through the wood.

Eyeing the door, the man backed away down the hall. His face was changing, softening. He examined the walls, the chandelier, the doors, with a strange, wide-eyed expression of . . . what? Shock? Wonder? Fear? Hunger? Judy couldn't tell.

He made his way to the door at the end of the hallway, the one Aunt Nora couldn't open. He tried the locked doorknob for a moment, then gave the door a sharp kick.

It smacked against the inner wall as it opened. The man wandered in, gazing around. Judy and Peter crept out of the linen closet. Hugging against the wall, they tiptoed to the end and peeked in.

Like the rest of the house, it was full of stuff. Unlike the other rooms, nothing was covered with protective sheets. A desk, a bed, sports gear on the wall, bookshelves — all of it was covered with thick dust, left exactly the way it had been when the family moved.

Alan Parrish's room, Judy thought. She felt a sadness for the boy she never knew.

The man was standing near an old mirror that was propped against the wall. His fingers over the frame, leaving a snaky

Frantically Judy skimmed the instructions: " 'Welcome to the safari' . . . let's see, 'You roll the dice to move your token . . . doubles gets another turn . . . the first player to reach the end and yell "Jumanji" wins, and . . .' " Suddenly she blanched. "Uh-oh . . . 'Adventurers beware: Do not begin unless you intend to finish. The exciting consequences of the game will vanish only when a player has reached Jumanji and called out its name.' *Whaaaaat?*"

A loud slam gave them both a start.

The front door.

They raced to the broken window. Through it they could see the monkeys marching out of the house — two by two, fanning out in all directions, taking to the streets.

Too weird. Peter knelt over the board and began folding it back up.

"Wait!" Judy said. "The instructions say if we finish the game, it'll all go away. We'd better do it, or Aunt Nora's going to pitch a fit!"

Peter wasn't budging.

"We'll get through it quickly," Judy insisted. "Just keep rolling the dice. I mean, there's no *skill* involved."

Peter thought a moment. With a reluctant sigh, he opened the board and held out the dice to Judy.

70

67

"No, no, no, you rolled doubles!" Judy reminded him. "You get another turn."

Peter's hand trembled as he let the dice spill to the board.

The first landed on a five, the second on a three.

Eight.

As Peter's token slid ahead, his message materialized:

His fangs are sharp; he likes your taste;
Your party better move, posthaste.

"Posthaste?" Judy repeated.

Plink.

Behind them, a piano key tinkled.

Goose bumps pricked Judy's arms. She and Peter slowly rose and looked toward the piano.

They saw a tail swishing across the keys. And an enormous silhouette rise onto its haunches above the piano's top. They heard the ugly noise as it stepped on the keys, lowering itself to the floor.

But it took a while for the reality to sink in.

It wasn't often you saw a lion in an attic. Especially a lion the size of a bus.

"RRROOOOOAAAR!"

Judy and Peter flew out the door and dashed downstairs.

The lion leaped from the spiral staircase,

barely missing a chandelier. With a heavy *whump,* it landed in the second-floor hallway.

Now it was right in front of Judy and Pet
And it looked very hungry.

Howling with terror, they ran the op
way.

And came face-to-face with a
knife-wielding caveman.

His hair was long and matt
crazed and piercing. He was dre
skins and a hat made from a t
knife looked homemade, with

"Yeeeeeaggh!" Judy a
back, stumbling toward the

The man pushed the
into an open linen close

The man and lio
and unmoving. Wit
threw his knife. I
beast's feet.

The lion sp
from the close

But the
and grabbe

The
slid — r

T
the

Frantically Judy skimmed the instructions: " 'Welcome to the safari' . . . let's see, 'You roll the dice to move your token . . . doubles gets another turn . . . the first player to reach the end and yell "Jumanji" wins, and . . .' " Suddenly she blanched. "Uh-oh . . . 'Adventurers beware: Do not begin unless you intend to finish. The exciting consequences of the game will vanish only when a player has reached Jumanji and called out its name.' *Whaaaaat?*"

A loud slam gave them both a start.

The front door.

They raced to the broken window. Through it they could see the monkeys marching out of the house — two by two, fanning out in all directions, taking to the streets.

Too weird. Peter knelt over the board and began folding it back up.

"Wait!" Judy said. "The instructions say if we finish the game, it'll all go away. We'd better do it, or Aunt Nora's going to pitch a fit!"

Peter wasn't budging.

"We'll get through it quickly," Judy insisted. "Just keep rolling the dice. I mean, there's no *skill* involved."

Peter thought a moment. With a reluctant sigh, he opened the board and held out the dice to Judy.

67

"No, no, no, you rolled doubles!" Judy reminded him. "You get another turn."

Peter's hand trembled as he let the dice spill to the board.

The first landed on a five, the second on a three.

Eight.

As Peter's token slid ahead, his message materialized:

His fangs are sharp; he likes your taste;
Your party better move, posthaste.

"Posthaste?" Judy repeated.

Plink.

Behind them, a piano key tinkled.

Goose bumps pricked Judy's arms. She and Peter slowly rose and looked toward the piano.

They saw a tail swishing across the keys. And an enormous silhouette rise onto its haunches above the piano's top. They heard the ugly noise as it stepped on the keys, lowering itself to the floor.

But it took a while for the reality to sink in.

It wasn't often you saw a lion in an attic. Especially a lion the size of a bus.

"RRROOOOOAAAR!"

Judy and Peter flew out the door and dashed downstairs.

The lion leaped from the spiral staircase,

barely missing a chandelier. With a heavy *whump,* it landed in the second-floor hallway.

Now it was right in front of Judy and Peter. And it looked very hungry.

Howling with terror, they ran the opposite way.

And came face-to-face with a bearded, knife-wielding caveman.

His hair was long and matted, his eyes crazed and piercing. He was dressed in animal skins and a hat made from a tortoise shell. His knife looked homemade, with a bone handle.

"Yeeeeeagggh!" Judy and Peter jumped back, stumbling toward the lion.

The man pushed them aside. They jumped into an open linen closet and hid.

The man and lion faced each other, tense and unmoving. With a sudden growl, the man threw his knife. It lodged in the floor, at the beast's feet.

The lion sprang at the man's throat. Peeking from the closet, Judy cringed.

But the man leaped high on powerful legs and grabbed onto the chandelier.

The lion landed on the hallway rug and slid — right into Aunt Nora's bedroom.

The man jumped to the bare floor, ran to the door, and kicked it shut. From inside, the lion bellowed. With a loud *crrraaaaack*, five sharp claws smashed through the wood.

Eyeing the door, the man backed away down the hall. His face was changing, softening. He examined the walls, the chandelier, the doors, with a strange, wide-eyed expression of . . . what? Shock? Wonder? Fear? Hunger? Judy couldn't tell.

He made his way to the door at the end of the hallway, the one Aunt Nora couldn't open. He tried the locked doorknob for a moment, then gave the door a sharp kick.

It smacked against the inner wall as it opened. The man wandered in, gazing around.

Judy and Peter crept out of the linen closet. Keeping against the wall, they tiptoed to the room and peeked in.

Like the rest of the house, it was full of stuff. But unlike the other rooms, nothing was covered with protective sheets. A desk, a bed, sports posters on the wall, bookshelves — all of it was coated with thick dust, left exactly the way it must have been when the family moved.

Alan Parrish's room, Judy thought. She felt a tug of sadness for the boy she never knew.

The hairy man was standing near an old Schwinn bike that was propped against the wall. He ran his fingers over the frame, leaving a snaky trail in the dust. Despite his savage appearance, his touch seemed soft and loving.

Walking to the back of the room, he opened a closet full of boy's clothes. He fingered a torn, dark-stained shirt that hung on a hook. Then, as if he were in a trance, he went to the dresser and examined a photo of a smiling man and woman.

He stared for a long time, then looked into the mirror that hung above the dresser.

Turning suddenly, he stared at Judy and Peter.

His lips moved. At first, no sound came out. Then he spoke, thickly and awkwardly, but in English. Judy and Peter leaned forward to hear his words.

"Diiid sommmme . . . body roll a five or an eight?"

CHAPTER 11

A *five or an eight?*
        Peter gulped. He released his neck muscles and nodded.

"AAAAAAAAAAGGGGHHHH!"

With an earsplitting cry, the man pounced on him.

Peter cried out, but he was too late to escape. The man lifted him and jumped up and down, whooping and dancing with joy, spinning around. Laughing.

Peter was petrified. Was this some kind of tribal ritual? A dance before the kill?

The man suddenly dropped him. His rapturous smile vanished. With catlike reflexes, he dashed down the stairs to the first floor.

Judy and Peter ran after him. He was bounding in and out of rooms, looking around crazily.

"Mom! Dad!" he cried out. "Where are you? I'm home!"

Peter's jaw dropped.

Judy narrowed her eyes at the man. "You're not . . . Alan Parrish, are you?"

The man spun around. "Who are you?"

"I'm Judy and he's Peter. We live here now. This house has been empty for years. Everyone thought you were dead."

Alan Parrish stared back, his face lined with confusion. Judy figured him to be about Aunt Nora's age, maybe older, but she could see the soul of a boy behind his confused eyes. "So . . ." he said uncertainly. "Where are my parents?"

Judy and Peter exchanged a glance. "We don't know," Judy replied softly. "Sorry."

Without another word, Alan turned and ran out the front door.

Judy and Peter scrambled after him. He ran across the lawn, then turned, gazing in amazement at the house. His skins flapping in the breeze, he backed into the street.

SCREEEEEEE . . .

A patroling police cruiser fishtailed toward him, trying to stop. Alan whirled around and leaped.

He landed on the hood with a loud thump.

A police officer climbed out of the car. He

73

was a solidly built man, going gray around the temples. And he was not amused.

"*Get down off my car!*" he commanded.

Alan hopped to the street.

"Step up on the sidewalk," the policeman ordered, closely examining his car's hood. As far as Judy could see, Alan had left no damage, but the officer used his jacket sleeve to wipe the area touched by Alan's feet. This was a man who paid attention to detail.

Alan leaned over the policeman's shoulder. He seemed stunned by the car's appearance. "What year is it?" he asked.

"It's brand-new!" the policeman retorted.

"No, I mean, what year is it now?"

The policeman glowered at Alan as if he were a nut case. Quickly Judy stepped forward and said, "Uh . . . nineteen ninety-five, remember?"

"You have some I.D.?" the policeman asked doubtfully, looking at Alan's outfit.

But Alan was muttering to himself, deep in thought. "Ninety-five minus sixty-nine . . . *twenty-six years?*"

"Yeah, I know, it's in your other pants, right?" the policeman growled. "You from around here?"

"Yes," Alan replied, "but I've been in Jumanji."

"Indonesia," Judy interjected. "He was in the Peace Corps."

Alan's eyes were now fixed on the policeman's badge, on which was printed the name BENTLEY.

He searched the man's face, suddenly familiar. "*Carl* Bentley?"

Officer Bentley turned to Judy. "Is this man related to you?"

"Yes, sir," Judy lied. "He's our . . . uncle."

Behind Officer Bentley's back, two Jumanji monkeys loped down the street and climbed into his cruiser.

Alan spotted them. Gritting his teeth, he let out a loud lionlike roar.

Officer Bentley spun around. The monkeys ducked to the car floor.

"Is he okay . . . upstairs?" Officer Bentley asked Judy.

"He suffered a head injury a few months ago," Judy answered. "You know how when you're on a train, you're not supposed to stick anything out the window? Well —"

Vvvrrrrrooooom!

The cruiser started up. As it tore away from

the curb, a gunshot from inside blasted a hole through the car's roof.

As it careened away, the sound of chattering laughter filled the street.

"Whaaaat?" Officer Bentley sprinted after his car, shouting over his shoulder, "Don't you go anywhere!"

Alan immediately took off in the opposite direction.

"Wait a minute," Judy called out. "Where are you going?"

"To find my parents!" Alan replied.

"Hey, what about the game?" Judy shouted. "It says we have to finish!"

"Go ahead, finish!" Alan said, disappearing around a corner.

Judy and Peter sprinted after him. Halfway up the street, they passed a mailman. He had stopped in the middle of the sidewalk and was sneezing like crazy, desperately trying to scratch his back.

Judy and Peter both gave him a look, and they nearly lost sight of Alan. Barreling around into Main Street, they finally caught up.

Alan was standing, stock-still, at the intersection with Elm. The town square was a drab, run-down strip of pawn shops, liquor stores, and cheap diners. Many of the storefronts were boarded up with broken planks. Across the street stood the lopsided shell of a car, stripped of its parts. Ragged piles of trash formed small whirlpools in the wind.

Alan stepped into the intersection, as if trying to remember something. A gang of black-leather-clad bikers zoomed by, nearly running him over.

Alan jumped back onto the sidewalk. Then he ran into the town green and stood at the base of an old statue. Under the scrawl of graffiti, the name GENERAL ANGUS PARRISH was barely visible. A beer can had been impaled on the tip of the general's sword.

"What happened?" Alan muttered to himself.

He darted suddenly away from the square, up Mill Road. He seemed to glide, with an effortless, loping gait that was way too fast for Judy and Peter.

Huffing and puffing, they met up with him at an abandoned construction site, near an overgrown marble mile marker.

The site was no more than a huge pit. A few concrete forms poked out of a thicket of wild vines and weeds. Scraggly trees and bushes had sprung up from the bottom. It was as if the crew had just stopped working one day and never returned.

Judy hoped this place was the end of Alan's search.

But Alan kept going, toward a crumbling brick factory just beyond an empty, weed-choked parking lot.

In front of the building, riddled with bullet holes, was a rusty sign that said PARRISH SHOES: FOUR GENERATIONS OF QUALITY.

Alan looked heartbroken. His eyes grew heavy and moist as he walked in the factory's front door.

In the semidarkness, the rotted hulks of old equipment stood like dinosaur skeletons. Birds flew among the rafters, toward thick nests tucked into the corners. From gaping holes in the ceiling, water dripped into lime-encrusted puddles.

Alan stooped to the floor and picked up an old, flattened box. He could barely make out the faded PARRISH SHOES logo on it. Clutching it to his chest like an injured pet, he asked, "Where is everybody? There used to be hundreds of — " He turned to face Judy and Peter. "My dad made shoes here. The best shoes in New England."

Alan's eyes darted upward, to an office door on a balcony. He ran up the metal stairs, two by two.

The words SAM PARRISH, PRESIDENT were stenciled on the frosted glass. Through it, Alan saw the silhouette of a man.

The man's feet were on a desk. His hands rested behind his head. And in his mouth was a pipe.

Alan's face lit up with joy. *Yes! He was alive!* Eagerly he pushed the door open.

CHAPTER 12

The man in the seat spun around.

His hair was white, his face sunken and grizzled. On the floor beside him, among mounds of trash, was a sleeping cot. A pot of water boiled on a propane stove against the wall.

Alan slumped. "I'm sorry, I thought you were someone else."

The face was totally unfamiliar. He was a homeless man. Taking refuge in the old office. Sitting at Mr. Parrish's desk.

Alan turned to leave, then changed his mind. He eyed the old man hopefully. "Do you know what happened to the shoe factory?"

Looking at Alan's raggedy outfit, the man seemed to relax. "It folded, like everything else in this town." He held out a coffee cup. "It's cold out there. You want some?"

Alan shook his head. "What about the Parrishes?" he pressed on.

"After their kid disappeared, they put everything they had into finding him," the old man explained. "Their money, their time, their *everything*. After a while, Sam stopped coming to work. He just quit caring. Some of us tried to keep the place going, but I guess we just didn't have the Parrish touch."

He reached into a pile of clothes and pulled out a pair of flared, polyester safari-suit pants that were so disgusting Judy almost laughed. "Here," the man offered, "these'll go better with that coat."

Alan put them on absently. "Are the Parrishes still around?"

"Yeah," the man said with an odd smile. "They're over on Adams Street."

Beaming with joy, Alan ducked out of the office.

Judy's legs ached from the running. She and Peter tailed him out of the building, but Alan left them in the dust of Mill Road.

They finally found Alan on Adams Street, just off the town square.

He was on his knees, before two tombstones in a cemetery. As Judy came closer, she could read the names carved into the marble: *Samuel*

Alan Parrish, June 18, 1921 — May 6, 1991; and *Carol Anne Parrish, November 20, 1930 — August 19, 1991.*

Judy and Peter kept a respectful distance. Wiping his eyes, Alan placed his tortoise-shell hat gently on his parents' graves.

When he noticed Judy and Peter, he hid his face in his hands and cried, "I wish this family didn't exist!"

"Our parents are dead, too," Judy said softly. "They were in the Middle East, negotiating peace, when — "

Peter elbowed her sharply. He stepped toward Alan and uttered the first words he'd said to anyone besides Judy since the accident. "Our dad was in advertising."

Alan's and Peter's eyes met. For a moment, neither said a word.

Then Alan stood up and strode away.

"There he goes again," Judy said. "Come on."

Alan was only walking, but the two kids had to jog to keep pace. They trailed him down a path that wound through the old graveyard. "Listen," Judy called out, "I know you're upset and all, but I was hoping you could help my brother and me finish the game."

"Sorry," Alan snapped.

They passed a woman who was kneeling

solemnly at a grave. Peter noticed she was scratching herself madly.

Just like the mailman. Strange.

"You could be a little grateful," Judy was saying. "Without us, you'd still be stuck in there."

"I'm forever in your debt for getting me out," Alan replied, "but it wouldn't make a whole lot of sense if the first thing I did was to go and get stuck in there again, would it? *No!* I've got too much catching up to do."

"There's a lion in my aunt's bedroom!" Judy shouted.

"Call a zoo!" Alan shot back. "I'm out of the lion business."

As they walked out of the graveyard and onto Main Street, a wailing ambulance approached. Left and right, cars pulled to the curb.

Except one. It was a convertible, veering all over the street.

Alan, Judy, and Peter stopped to watch. The ambulance swerved. The car swerved in the same direction.

EEEEEEEEEE . . .

Tires squealed. With a sickening crunch of metal, the car and the ambulance sideswiped one another.

They both lurched to a stop at the curb.

The ambulance doors swung open and two paramedics rushed out. One went around back to get a stretcher. The second ran to the car, opened the driver's door, and pulled out a woman.

She was shaking violently and scratching. Her face was greenish-yellow and she was covered with a sheen of sweat.

"We got another one, Larry!" the paramedic called out.

"That's over fifty of them!" the other one said, laying the stretcher by the woman. "What's going on around here?"

As the men lifted the woman onto the stretcher, she tossed back her head and sneezed.

Judy recognized her at once. It was Ms. Winston, the real-estate woman. "Hey, isn't that — ?"

"Quiet!" Alan blurted out. He cocked his head to one side, an intent look in his eyes. "Do you hear that?"

"Hear what?" Judy asked.

Judy and Peter listened carefully but could hear nothing unusual. Alan's eyes, however, were widening with terror.

He pushed the two kids toward Ms. Winston's car. "Quick! Move it!"

All three of them piled into the front seat through the open driver's door. Alan slammed the door shut and clutched the steering wheel. "Think!" he urged. "What came out of the game before me?"

"There was the lion," Judy said, "a bunch of monkeys, and — "

A giant mosquito dropped from the sky onto the hood of the car.

"*That!*" Peter shouted.

Tap-tap . . . tap-tap-tap . . . The mosquito poked the windshield with its stinger.

"Don't worry," Alan said, "he can't get us in here."

The mosquito buzzed away, out of sight. "See?" Alan said with a cocky smile. "We're fine."

Rrrrrrip! The mosquito's stinger slashed through the convertible top.

Judy and Peter screamed.

As they cowered against the dashboard, the stinger thrashed around for a while, then withdrew.

"We're safe," Alan assured them. "Those things'll make you sick if they bite you, but if we go home and stay inside, we'll be okay."

BzzzzzZZZZZZ — smack!

The mosquito dive-bombed the windshield, cracking the glass.

"*How?*" Judy's question was an anguished shout.

Alan was examining the steering column, which still had keys in it. "Do either of you know how to drive?" he asked.

Judy and Peter both shook their heads.

"Okay, okay, no problem. Give me some room here. My dad let me back the car down the driveway once, and he used to let me sit on his lap and steer all the time. It's been a while, but — "

He turned the ignition key. With a roar, the car started.

"Okaaaaay!" Alan exclaimed. "On our way!"

Judy and Peter quickly fastened their seat belts.

Alan pressed his foot on the accelerator. The engine revved loudly, but the car stayed put.

Alan tried pressing a button to the left of the steering wheel. Nothing happened. He tried a lever. The windshield wipers began swinging. A knob. The radio blasted. Another button. The convertible top began to lower.

"Alan!" Judy cried. "The top!"

As the top folded neatly behind them, Alan sat there, dumbfounded.

BzzzzzZZZZZZZZ . . .

Judy looked up. The mosquito was dropping from high above. Fast.

She did the only thing she could.

Closed her eyes and screamed.

CHAPTER 13

Peter leaned over her. He yanked the gearshift down to drive.

The car peeled away, tires screeching.

Judy opened her eyes and looked over her shoulder. The mosquito landed on the blacktop and bounced.

Alan swung the steering wheel wildly. The car hopped a curb and headed for a stop sign.

Judy and Peter braced themselves. They jolted forward as the car hit.

The sign folded, slapping to the ground. Alan drove on, swerving into the street, skidding from one curb to the other.

He turned hard onto Jefferson Street.

EEEEEEEE . . . crrrack!

Down went the neighbor's fence.

EEEEEEEE . . . thwwock! Judy and Peter's mailbox.

Alan slammed his foot on the brake. Judy thought her seat belt was going to slice her in half. She and Peter gripped the dashboard.

The car banked to a stop at the curb.

Alan exhaled hard. "Piece of cake," he said, turning off the ignition.

He climbed out of the car and scurried into the house.

For a moment, neither Judy nor Peter could move. *Alive. I am alive.* Judy kept repeating the words in her mind. As if to convince herself.

Slowly she and Peter peeled their white-knuckled hands from the dashboard.

They found Alan in the attic. A trunk filled with men's clothes lay open at his feet. He was standing before a mirror, holding up a wrinkled shirt to his torso. He seemed to be examining it for the fit — but also admiring it tenderly. Lost in his own world.

It must have belonged to his dad, Judy realized.

Feeling a tug of sadness, she thought about leaving him alone. But she spotted the Jumanji board on the floor and remembered its message.

The exciting consequences of the game will

vanish only when a player has reached Jumanji and called out its name. Some exciting consequences — lions, a monkey army, attack mosquitoes that carried an itching disease.

They needed to finish. More than anything else. And they needed Alan to protect them.

Judy held up the game and gently called out, "Alan? So when are you going to help us play?"

Startled, Alan turned around to face her. When he saw the game, he backed away. Even in the attic's dim light, she could see his face go pale. When he spoke, his voice was an anguished whisper. "You keep that thing away from me!"

"But we've got to hurry!" Judy insisted. "Our aunt's going to be home."

Alan scooped up some clothes from the trunk and swept past Judy and her brother. "Good. Then I can inform her that she's the ex-owner of this house. You realize that with my parents gone, this place is mine now, don't you?"

He bounded down the attic stairs, leaving Judy as speechless as her brother.

"How's the hot water here these days?" Alan called over his shoulder. "Did anyone replace that old boiler?"

Still holding the game board, Judy ran after him, with Peter close behind. Alan ducked into the second-floor bathroom and slammed the door in their faces.

"What do you think those monkeys are going to do to the ecosystem around here?" Judy shouted. "*Hello?*"

Alan began humming out of tune, to a background of running water and snipping scissors. Exasperated, Judy and Peter sat on the hallway floor. Behind them, they could hear the lion snuffling around in Aunt Nora's bedroom, ripping sheets and crashing against furniture.

When the bathroom door opened, Alan was dressed in his dad's casual clothes — a tweed jacket, checked shirt, and khaki pants. He'd lopped off most of his hair in uneven chunks, and his shaven face was so full of cuts it made Judy wince.

"What do you want?" Alan said with a frown. "I've never shaved before."

Once again he ran past them. They tailed him downstairs to the kitchen. There, Judy felt her stomach turn.

The monkeys had destroyed the place. The walls and floors were full of trampled, rotting, half-chewed food. Alan was collecting chunks of it in a big bowl.

"How about, Peter and I play the game, and you just sort of watch?" Judy suggested.

"No, thanks." Alan eyed a squashed doughnut and added it to his collection. "I've seen it. Besides, I don't plan farther ahead than my next meal. I learned that the hard way."

"Well, if you aren't going to help us, what *are* you going to do?" Judy asked.

Alan thought about that for a moment. "I guess I'll just pick up where I left off," he said, reaching for the refrigerator door. "I wonder if Mrs. Nedermeyer still teaches sixth grade . . ."

"EEEEEEE!" A monkey leaped out of the fridge, shivering and angry-looking.

Alan jumped away, dropping his bowl. The monkey chattered at him furiously, then loped away.

Alan cleared his throat and tried a nonchalant smile, covering his fright. But his face was bright red with embarrassment.

Which gave Peter an idea. "Come on, Judy," he spoke up. "He's not going to help us. He's afraid."

"*What?*" Alan exclaimed. "What did you say?"

"You're afraid," Peter replied with a shrug. "Hey, it's okay to be afraid."

"I'm *not* afraid!" Alan replied.

"Prove it."

"I don't need to prove anything to you!"

Peter turned toward his sister. "Let's set it up in the living room."

As Peter started to walk toward the kitchen door, Alan stood in front of him. "Listen, you don't know what you're getting into."

"Whatever it is, we'll handle it ourselves," Peter said. "We don't need you. Come on, Judy."

"You think monkeys and mosquitoes and lions are bad?" Alan sneered. "That's kid stuff. I've seen things that would give you nightmares the rest of your life. Things you can't even imagine — snakes as long as a school bus, spiders the size of bulldogs, things that hunt in the jungle at night. Things you don't even see, you just hear them running and . . . *eating*. It's okay to be afraid? You don't know what fear is. Believe me, you won't last five minutes without me!"

Peter locked eyes with Alan for a long moment. "So, you *are* going to help us play?"

Growling with frustration, Alan stalked out of the kitchen. "All right, all right!"

Judy grinned admiringly at her brother. "Peter, that was cool."

"Reverse psychology," Peter replied. "Dad used to pull it on me all the time."

They jogged into the living room. There,

Alan was pulling all the drapes shut, casting the room in semidarkness. When he returned to Judy and Peter, his face was lined with fear.

Judy opened the game board. The tokens were still in their places. Picking up the dice, she said, "Ready?"

"Ready," Peter replied.

"Ready," Alan mumbled.

"Okay, here I go!" Judy tossed the dice onto the board.

They all stared at her token. It stood completely still.

"I'll try again." Judy rolled a second time.

Nothing.

"Alan, it's not working," Judy said.

A realization crept slowly across Alan's face. *"Oh, no!"* He sprang up from his seat. "It's not your turn!"

"I rolled first," Judy explained, "then Peter twice, because he got doubles. Now it's mine again."

"No, look." Alan pointed to Judy's and Peter's tokens. "If these two are yours, whose are the others? *One* of them's mine." His eyes became suddenly distant and sad. "You're playing the game I started in nineteen sixty-nine."

"So whose turn is it?" Judy asked.

94

"The person I was playing with," Alan said softly.

"Well? Who was that?" Judy pressed on.

Alan slumped over to the window. His eyes grew moist as he gazed outside. Then he spoke up, in a choked whisper.

"Sarah Whittle."

CHAPTER 14

MADAM SERENA
PSYCHIC READINGS
BY APPOINTMENT ONLY

The wooden sign was warped and cracked, the words faded. As Alan surveyed the house that had once belonged to the Whittles, his face looked hollow and dismayed.

Thick, gnarled trees loomed overhead, casting the house and its scraggly lawn in deep shadow. Weeds grew between cracks in the walkway, which led to a sagging porch.

"This place gives me the creeps," Peter said.

"I knew she wouldn't still be here," Alan said with a sigh.

"Well, let's at least ask," Judy suggested. "Maybe she'll know where Sarah went."

They walked to the front door, and Judy knocked.

Alan gazed around with a wistful smile. "We used to play right here on this porch. It seemed a lot bigger in those days."

"Hello?" came a muffled female voice from behind the front door.

"Can you help us?" Judy asked loudly. "We're — "

"Do you have an appointment?" the voice interrupted.

"No," Judy replied, "we're just trying to find someone."

"Madam Serena won't see you right now!" came the impatient reply.

"Well, maybe you can help us," Alan spoke up.

The door creaked slowly open. A woman stood squinting at them, her blond hair tousled and her eyes puffy, as if she'd just awakened.

"We're looking for someone who used to live here," Alan informed her.

"I've lived here all my life," the woman snapped.

"Then you must know Sarah Whittle," Judy said.

"Wh-why . . . do you want Sarah Whittle?"

Alan's eyes were as big as baseballs. *"Sarah?"*

"I — " The woman fidgeted. "I don't go by that name anymore."

"Sarah *Whittle?*" The name burst from Alan's mouth in a joyous shout. He stepped toward her, grinning from ear to ear.

Sarah backed away. "What do you want?"

"When you were thirteen, you played a game with a kid down the street," Alan said. "The game with the drums."

"How do you kn-know about that?" Sarah was trembling uncontrollably now.

"Because I was there, Sarah."

She sucked in a short gasp. Her sleepy eyes were alert and open now. *"Alan?"* she whispered.

Before he could answer, she fell to the floor in a dead faint.

It took Alan a few minutes to revive her into semiconsciousness. Propping her left arm around his shoulders, and her right arm around Judy's, Alan slowly led them all back to the old Parrish house.

While she was still groggy, Peter ran into the kitchen and brought back some lemonade the monkeys hadn't destroyed. Alan shoved the game under the coffee table. Better to ease her into the past.

98

After a few sips, Sarah revived. Ignoring everyone, she went right for the living room phone and quickly tapped out a number.

A muffled beep sounded from the receiver.

"Yes, Doctor Boorstein, it's Sarah Whittle calling," she said. "I might need to have my dosage checked. You know the event we've been talking about for the past two decades or so? The one that didn't really happen? Well, I seem to be having another episode involving that little boy who didn't really disappear. I'm sitting in his living room drinking lemonade. I'd be very interested in your interpretation. Please call me back at your next opportunity. Thank you."

After leaving Alan's phone number, she hung up and looked nervously around the house. "He'll call me back at ten minutes before the hour."

"Okay." Alan took a deep breath. "Well, while we're waiting . . ." He reached under the coffee table and pulled out the game.

Sarah leaped to her feet and shrieked. *"Get that thing away from me!"*

"You have to help us finish the game, Sarah," Judy insisted.

"No, I don't!" Sarah turned to Alan, red-eyed. "I've spent over two thousand hours in therapy convincing myself that thing doesn't exist! I made it all up about you turning into smoke and disappearing into the game because whatever *really* happened was just too awful!"

"Yeah, it was awful," Alan said with a nod. "But it was real."

"No! Your father murdered you and chopped you into little pieces and hid you in the walls!"

"My *father* did that?"

Sarah nodded.

"Sarah, you knew my father. He could barely *hug* me, let alone chop me into pieces."

"Well, it's *always* the repressed types who —"

"Listen, twenty-six years ago we started something, and now we're all going to finish it. And guess what?" Alan grabbed the dice and put them into Sarah's palms. "It's your turn."

Sarah jumped back. "I won't play!"

Alan leaned into her. "You *will* play!"

"Just try and make me," Sarah hissed, her teeth bared like an animal under attack.

Alan slammed the game board down on the coffee table. "All right, just give me the dice and get out of here!"

Judy's heart sank. Beside her, Peter looked as if he would cry.

Alan held his palm out to Sarah. She reached out and dropped the dice.

With lightning reflexes, Alan pulled his hand back. The dice clattered to the game board.

"AAAAAAAAGGGCHHH!" Sarah howled. "How could you *do* that?"

"Sorry." Alan grinned. "Law of the jungle."

The drumming began, soft and menacing. Sarah's token slid forward on the path.

Sarah sank onto the floor. "When I think of all the energy I've spent visualizing you as a radiant spirit . . ."

Her message began to materialize in the circle. "Go on," Judy urged. "Read it."

"Twenty-two years of Dr. Boorstein down the drain," Sarah rambled on. "All I can say is it's a good thing I had health insurance — "

"*Read it!*" Alan commanded.

Sarah looked tentatively at the board. " 'They grow much faster than bamboo,' " she read. " 'Take care or they'll come after you.' "

A chunk of plaster fell from above and smashed onto the game board.

Alan, Sarah, Judy, and Peter looked up. A green vine was poking through a crack in the ceiling. It spiraled downward, spewing more plaster.

"No!" Sarah cried. "No! Don't let this be happening!"

Crrrrrrack! Another vine burst through a painting on the wall.

Dzzzzzzt! Sparks flew as another one snaked out of an electrical outlet.

From the moldings, the sofa cushions, the fireplace — the vines twined around furniture, growing instant leaves and buds.

"Stay away from the walls!" Alan warned.

Judy watched in awe as a bud sprouted into a lush, purple blossom. "Wow, they're beautiful!"

As she reached out to touch one, Alan shouted, "Don't! They shoot poison barbs!"

"Heyyyy!" Peter suddenly cried out.

A vine had wrapped around his ankle. It yanked him to the floor, pulling him under the carpet.

"Peter!" Judy screamed.

The vine was fast. Peter shot across the room, a moving, shrieking lump.

"Get him!" Alan bellowed.

He, Sarah, and Judy gave chase. The vine pulled Peter out the other end of the rug. He twisted, shook his leg, grasped for handholds. But the vine's grip was viselike. It dragged him toward an antique mahogany breakfront with glass doors.

The doors shattered open. Through the jagged opening, a monstrous green pod grew outward. It lunged toward Peter, opening to reveal long, glistening teeth!

CHAPTER 15

"**N**O-O-O-O-O-O-O!"
Peter's shouts echoed through the vaulted room. He flailed desperately.

The pod's jaws stretched wider. Saliva bubbled up from within, dripping to the floor.

Alan threw himself across the room. He grabbed Peter's free ankle. Judy and Sarah dived for Peter's two arms.

All three of them planted their feet firmly and pulled. The vine stretched like a thick rubber cable.

But it held fast. Judy felt her feet sliding. Alan's arm muscles, thick-sinewed and powerful from years of jungle living, were helpless against the vines.

They were all about to be plant food.

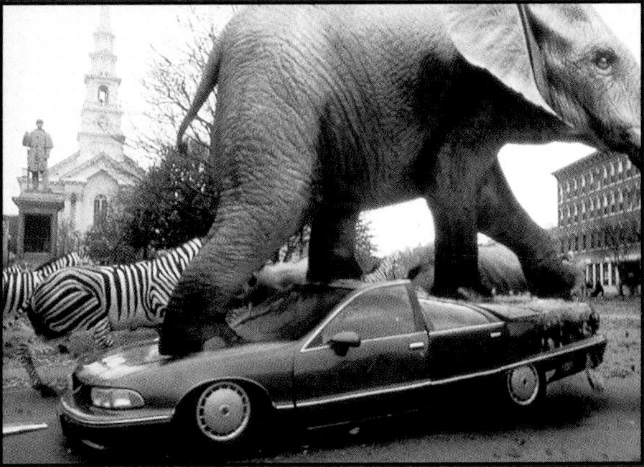

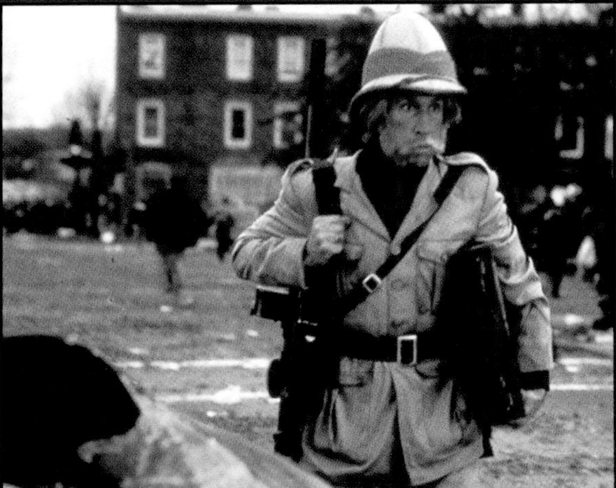

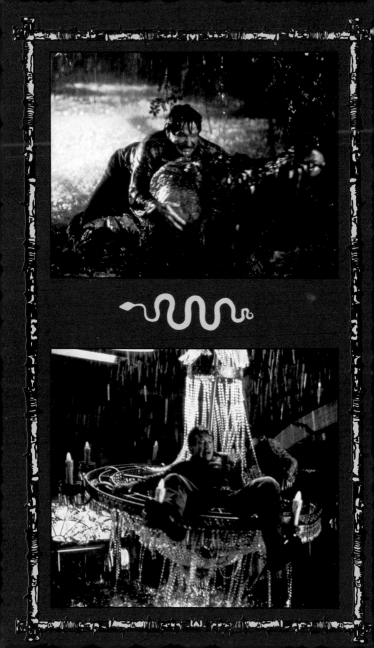

Alan's eyes darted around the room wildly. Then, without warning, he let go.

Judy, Sarah, and Peter lunged forward.

Alan sprinted toward the fireplace. He reached above the mantel for the glass display case that contained the old saber.

Smashing the case to the floor, he grabbed the weapon.

The pod was drooling buckets as Peter's legs inched closer.

"Hyyyyyyyyeeeahhh!" Alan ran back, howling at the top of his lungs. He raised the saber high over his head.

Swwwooosh!

He brought it down hard.

With a loud snap, the vine split in two. Peter, Judy, and Sarah recoiled backward, tumbling across the living room.

The other half of the vine whipped back against the pod. A cloud of feathery seeds burst into the air.

Alan watched them float by. "Uh-oh," he said. "Whatever you do, *don't* open any windows. You wouldn't believe how fast these things grow."

Halfway across Brantford, Officer Carl Bentley trudged wearily down a quiet residential street.

Using his police instincts, he was tracking down his cruiser.

It wasn't hard. All he needed to do was follow the trail of sideswiped parked cars.

Turning a corner, he grimaced. "What the . . . ?"

His cruiser had come to a stop in the middle of the street. Its front grille was wrapped around an old maple tree. The roof and windows had been shot through with holes. And the doors and fenders showed all the dents from the slam dance along the way.

As he approached, he could hear his CB radio crackling.

Bentley pulled open the front door and climbed in. "Carl here," he said, picking up the mike.

"Where have you been?" barked the voice of the dispatcher, Lorraine Gordon. "We've got a serious animal-control situation on our hands."

"Get Stan or Willy on it," Bentley replied. "I'm heading over to the old Parrish place to investigate a suspicious character."

He jammed the mike back into its holder. Just to the left of it, his keys were dangling from the ignition. Saying a brief prayer, he turned them.

The engine started right up. Officer Bentley

smiled with relief. He threw the gear into reverse and backed up.

With a huge *RRRRIIIPPP*, the front separated from the tree.

In the back hall of the Parrish house, Alan threaded the end of a vine through the handles of the glass doors. He tied it in a complex knot, then backed away.

As the vine tried to pull away, it only made the knot tighter.

Alan smirked. "Try evolving a couple of million years. Maybe you'll figure it out."

Behind him, Sarah was tiptoeing toward the front of the house.

Alan turned and ran after her. He grabbed her arm from behind.

"Get your hands off me!" Sarah shouted.

"The game's not over yet, Sarah," Alan insisted.

"It is for me. Let me go!"

Alan dragged Sarah into the living room, grabbed the Jumanji board away from the glass shards, and then pulled her into the library.

Judy and Peter ran in after them.

"We'll finish the game right here," Alan commanded.

"This is so abusive," Sarah replied.

Judy scooped up the dice and handed them to Alan. "It's your turn."

"Last time I played this game, it ruined my life," Sarah grumbled.

Alan practically spat out his reply. "It ruined *your* life? 'In the jungle you must wait, until the dice read five or eight' — remember? But they didn't read five or eight for twenty-six years *because somebody stopped playing!*"

"I — I w-was just a kid," Sarah replied, shrinking away. "I couldn't handle it."

Judy stepped between them. "It's okay, Sarah. We're scared, too. But if we finish the game, it'll all go away."

"How do you know it won't happen again?" Sarah retorted. "How do *I* know *I* won't get stuck in the jungle?"

"Because," Alan cut in, "unlike some people, Sarah, *I* won't abandon my friends."

Sarah's face crumbled at the implied accusation.

"Neither will I," Judy said firmly.

Wordlessly, Peter thrust forward his fist. Judy placed hers on top of it. Alan added his.

All for one and one for all. Like the Three Musketeers.

They all looked at Sarah. "Well?" Alan asked.

Sarah swallowed. Her eyes grew distant and forlorn.

Finally, with a sigh, she put her fist on Alan's.

Under the stern gaze of General Parrish's bust, they held their arms for a grim moment of solidarity. Judy had never felt so nervous in her life.

As they released, Alan reached for the dice and rolled.

"I knew this was going to be a bad day," Sarah muttered.

"Oh, relax. All we have to do is roll with the punches, keep our heads, and everything's going to be fine." With a confident smile, Alan read his message in the center circle: " 'A hunter from the darkest wild, makes you feel . . . just like a . . .' "

Alan gulped. His smile vanished.

" 'Child,' " Judy continued reading. "*Child?*"

Alan had risen into a tense crouch, like a stalked animal. His brow was beaded with sweat as his eyes scanned the room. In a hushed and fearful voice, he rasped, "*Van Pelt . . .*"

Huh?

Judy gave Peter and Sarah a look.

KA-BOOOOOOM!

A shower of glass burst into the library from

the sunroom. A bullet whizzed through a cloud of whipped-up pod seeds. Alan ducked to the carpet.

The library wall took a solid hit, inches from his head.

"Get down!" Alan shouted.

The others dropped to the floor.

Through the opening stepped a burly, broad-shouldered hunter. Van Pelt was clad all in khaki. He wore a pith helmet on his head. His tight, grim mouth was framed by a bushy mustache and a granitelike jaw.

Pinning Alan with a cold, murderous stare, Van Pelt lifted his rifle, took aim, and fired!

CHAPTER 16

Alan scrambled out of the path of the bullet. It ripped into a wood molding. Yelping, Alan ran for the door.

"This isn't a footrace, lad!" Van Pelt shouted. "Stand up straight and let me pop you fair and square!"

Judy, Sarah, and Peter cowered in a corner. Van Pelt stomped into the room, his heavy jackboots smacking the floor like gunshots.

He trained his eyes on the three. Judy felt herself stiffen. Her legs trembled.

But the hunter turned away without the slightest shift of his expression and stalked after Alan.

Alan's footsteps echoed in the hallway, then stopped. Just outside the library door, Van Pelt raised his rifle.

Zzzzzzing! The saber sliced through the air

toward Van Pelt. With a loud rip, it tore through his jacket sleeve and lodged in the wall. His rifle jerked upward.

BLLLAAAMMMM! The shot blasted a hole in the ceiling.

Van Pelt checked his arm. Not even a flesh wound.

An evil, triumphant leer twisted the hunter's face. "You're a disgrace to the species, boy-o!" He yanked the saber out and lumbered down the hallway.

Alan tore out the front door. He flew across the lawn and into the street.

About a half block away, Officer Bentley's cruiser squealed to a halt.

Bentley jumped out. "Hey, you!"

But Alan kept running.

And Van Pelt took aim.

BLLLAAAMMMM! A tree branch snapped and fell inches from Alan.

Bentley ducked behind the cruiser's crumpled, open door. He quickly drew his pistol and pointed it at Van Pelt. "Drop the gun and get your hands up in the air!" he commanded.

Van Pelt calmly turned.

BLLAAMMMM! He shot out the cruiser's windshield.

BLLAAAMMM! BLLAAAMMM! The head-lights.

BLLAAAMMM!

A streetlamp burst directly over Bentley, sending a shower of glass onto his head.

Van Pelt now lined up Alan in his sights. Among the spacious, neatly trimmed lawns in the neighborhood, there was no place to hide.

A clear, easy shot. Van Pelt grinned.

Click.

Out of ammo. Van Pelt spat a curse.

Growling to himself in frustration, he clomped away after Alan.

Bentley cautiously poked his head above the cruiser door and surveyed the damage. "Oh, man . . ." he murmured.

Reaching inside, he snatched the CB receiver. "Lorraine, Lorraine!" he called. "Come in, Lorraine!"

"Yes, Carl," the dispatcher's voice responded.

"I'm in pursuit of an armed and dangerous Caucasian male, approximately one hundred sixty pounds, five-eleven, ten-gallon pith helmet, eighteen-nineties facial hair."

"Um, could you run that by me again?"

"No, I've got to go. I'll call in later."

He sat in the driver's seat and wiped away broken glass. The dented door creaked as he pulled it shut.

Throwing the cruiser into gear, he tore away from the curb.

In the house, Judy, Peter, and Sarah peered out from the small windows that flanked the front door.

"So," Sarah was explaining breathlessly, "even if Alan gets out of *this* situation, the same kind of thing is going to keep happening to him over and over. When you carry so much repressed anger, it attracts a lot of negative energy. He didn't end up in the jungle by accident. There *are* no accidents — "

"Whose turn is it?" asked Alan from behind them.

They all spun around. Alan was climbing in through the dining-room window.

He threw Sarah a broad smile. "So, where's the game?"

"Where we left it," Judy answered. "It's my turn next."

Alan darted toward the library. As the others ran after him, Sarah piped up, "You might have warned us that there was someone in there with a gun trying to kill us!"

"Is he the reason you didn't want to play?" Judy asked.

A grin of realization crept across Sarah's face. "Ohhhhhh, *he* didn't want to play, either? Well, well, well, Mister We-Started-Something-and-Now-We're-Going-to-Finish-It. What is it with you and that guy? A little personality problem?"

Alan took his place by the game board. "He's a hunter," he explained sharply. "He hunts. That's what he does. Right now, he's hunting *me.*"

"Why?" Sarah asked.

"I don't know," Alan replied. "He seems to find everything about me so offensive, you'd think he wouldn't want to waste his time."

Sarah nodded. "Have you ever tried sitting down and working out your differences?"

"Are you crazy? You can't talk to him. He's completely unreachable!"

"Don't you dare call me crazy!" Sarah erupted. "Everyone thinks I'm crazy, ever since I told the cops twenty-six years ago that you disappeared inside a board game!"

Alan rolled his eyes. "I wasn't calling you crazy. It was just a figure of — "

"Maybe I should roll," Judy interrupted. She

115

held out the dice between Alan and Sarah and shook hard. "Yoo-hoo, I'm rolling now!"

"You know what it's like to be known as the little girl who saw Alan Parrish murdered?" Sarah barreled onward. "You think anybody came to my fourteenth birthday party?"

"Not even *Billy Jessup?*" Alan sneered. "It sounds like his kind of party."

Sarah folded her arms stubbornly. "Billy who? I have no idea who you're talking about."

"Oh, come on, Madam Serena," Alan taunted. "I'm sure if you dig around in the lower reaches of your higher consciousness, you ought to be able to dredge up the memory of your boyfriend, Billy. You were the perfect match. *His* anger wasn't repressed — "

"Go ahead," Peter urged his sister. "Roll!"

Judy spilled the dice on the board. Her token moved up the path and a new message materialized:

Don't be fooled, it isn't thunder;
Staying put would be a blunder.

Oblivious, Sarah said, "You're talking about that guy who used to take your bicycle?"

"I'm talking about the guy you were at the movies with when you should have been finishing the game we started," Alan answered.

116

Peter noticed a plaster bust of Beethoven beginning to vibrate on a bookshelf.

Sarah narrowed her eyes at Alan. "You are *so* immature!"

"*I'm* immature? At least I — " Alan stopped abruptly. He cocked his ears. "Shut up! Listen!"

In the distance, a low rumbling noise was growing louder. Alan walked to the bookshelf and put his hand against it. The bust was shaking violently now.

Alan's eyes grew wide as ostrich eggs.

"*Stampeeeeeede!*" he cried out. Jumping to his feet, he pushed Peter, Sarah, and Judy across the room.

As they tumbled toward the front foyer, the library wall blew open.

 ooks exploded into the air in a plaster cloud. Wooden shelves became splinters.

Through the flying debris charged a . . . a crash of rhinoceroses.

That was the word. A *crash* of rhinos. Judy remembered it from school.

Funny how things like that came to you when you were about to die. About to be trampled in your own house.

Judy couldn't feel her feet touching the floor. She raced into the front foyer with Peter and Sarah, pushed from behind by Alan.

The rhinos were crashing.

Thundering.

Destroying everything in their wake.

Furniture hurtled out the side windows. Walls cracked.

Judy knew she was screaming, but she couldn't hear it. The stampede swallowed all sound.

The library doors burst off their hinges. Now the rhinos were charging down the front foyer.

Judy, Peter, Alan, and Sarah dived headlong into the parlor. Crouched against the wall, they felt the rush of air, the heat of the animals' skins, their stinking snorts.

As if it were paper, the west wall of the house ripped open. In a deafening rumble of hoofbeats, the rhinos tore onto the side lawn.

Behind the rhinos were elephants.

Behind the elephants were zebras.

As the last animal filed outside, dust settled over the parlor like a dying snowstorm. Judy gazed around at the devastation, not wanting to move, unwilling to risk a sudden attack from . . . what? Was there anything else? Hyenas? Water buffalos? Who knew, in the world of Jumanji?

Coughing out plaster dust, the four players unlocked their knees and stood. The parlor was a shambles, the walls gaping holes. The floor had sagged and cracked under the weight of the stampede.

But Alan had rescued the game board. It lay by their feet now, the tokens still standing where they'd been before.

What are we doing? Judy thought. The four of them brought this world into being. But could they possibly control it, or did it control them? Would the game destroy them before they could finish?

A flapping sound interrupted Judy's thoughts. From the hallway, a flock of pelicans flew into the room.

Their wings were huge, throwing parts of the room into shadow. They swooped by, heading straight for the broken wall.

"Hey!" Alan suddenly shouted.

The last pelican was diving for the Jumanji game. The bird closed its beak on the board and lifted it into the air.

Alan lunged after the pelican. "Don't let him get away!"

With a powerful thrust of its wings, the pelican flew into the foyer.

The four players gave chase. Over their heads, the pelican circled wildly. It turned toward the front hallway.

"Judy! Stop him!" Alan said.

Waving her arms, Judy ran to block its path. As it flew overhead, she jumped high.

Her fingers brushed the bottom of the board.

The pelican jerked away. Its eyes locked on

the smashed dining-room wall. Tipping its wings, it banked in that direction.

Alan pointed. "Sarah! Peter! Don't let him out!"

Sarah and Peter ran to the wall. They stood in front of the gaping hole the rhinos had made.

The pelican swerved toward Peter's head, picking up speed, dive-bombing . . .

Peter ducked.

The pelican escaped outside, soaring up beyond the trees, the game board firmly in its beak.

Alan scuttled past Peter, muttering angrily.

"I'm sorry," Peter whimpered. "He scared me."

But Alan was already outside, speeding across the lawn, looking skyward.

Peter looked crushed.

"Creep," Sarah muttered, scowling after Alan. She smiled sympathetically at Peter. "Don't worry. He's the last person you want as a role model."

Judy ran past them and shouted to Alan, "Where are you going?"

"*He'll head for the water!*" Alan called back.

Before the others could react, the telephone rang.

Judy ducked back inside. The ringing was

muffled, hidden. She rooted around the room and pulled a dusty phone from a pile of rubble.

Quickly she picked up the receiver. "Hello? . . . Oh, hi, Aunt Nora, I can't really talk right now. Well, a stampede of wild animals just ran through the house, a dozen monkeys destroyed the kitchen, and there's a really large lion trapped in your bedroom. . . . Right. . . . No, I understand. . . . Okay, 'bye."

Peter and Sarah looked at her impatiently.

"I'm grounded for another week," she announced as she led the others through the wall and across the lawn.

At the Brantford pawnshop on Main Street, Ralph Smigel and Lenny Creech sat behind the counter, snoozing.

Ralph's eyes sprang open as a man stopped in front of the display window.

A potential customer. Not something he and Ralph saw much of these days.

And what a specimen. Like Teddy Roosevelt, back from the dead. Complete with hunting rifle. Ready to stalk big game in the town square. Ralph chuckled. It took all types.

The dude examined the firearms section

of the window display, then headed into the shop. Ralph elbowed Lenny, who snorted awake.

"Morning," Ralph said to the guy.

Van Pelt didn't answer. He broke his rifle over the counter, sending a spent cartridge into the air.

Ralph caught it. Eyeing Van Pelt's khaki outfit, he asked, "You're not a postal worker, are you?"

"I am a hunter," Van Pelt replied.

Ralph tossed the cartridge to his partner. "Lenny, we carry these?"

Lenny held up the gleaming metal shell and smiled. "Kynock Nitroball . . . well, unfortunately, the company went belly-up in nineteen-oh-three."

"You want real ammo, you're going to have to get a real gun," Ralph said matter-of-factly to Van Pelt. "What do you hunt?"

"Animals," Van Pelt said.

Ralph reached under the counter and brought up a stack of papers. "Okay, I'll need a little info — driver's license, Social Security number, last three addresses. . . . You haven't done any time, have you?"

Without a word, Van Pelt reached into his

pocket and tossed a handful of gold coins onto the counter.

Ralph had to blink to believe what he was seeing. Visions of a new car and a Caribbean vacation danced in his head.

"Uh, these seem to be in order." Ralph shoved the paperwork under the counter. "So, you look like you got an eye for quality." Under his breath, he muttered to Lenny, "Watch the door."

Lenny scampered to the front door, locked it, and stood guard.

From a hidden area under the counter, Ralph pulled out an automatic sniper rifle with a telescopic sight and silencer.

Illegal? Oh, yeah. Ralph knew it. But he figured, okay, sure it could cause untold death and destruction, sure he'd be sent to the slammer if he were caught selling it.

But hey, the gold was on the table. And that was all that meant anything to Ralph.

He grinned at Van Pelt. "Top of the line. You love it, or what?"

Van Pelt looked through the sight. He swung the rifle around, taking in the store . . . the window . . . the street outside . . . the familiar, bashed-up police cruiser that had just parked at the curb ... the policeman inside, talking into his radio.

Van Pelt remembered that pest, all right. With an evil smile, he stomped out the door.

"Anyone asks you," Ralph called out, "you didn't get it here!"

But Van Pelt wasn't listening. His mind was already on Alan Parrish.

CHAPTER 18

"**O**w!" A branch whipped Judy's face. She pushed it aside and ran on, bushwhacking through the Brantford forest.

Peter tripped over a root, thudding to the ground. He knocked into Sarah's knee, throwing her against a pine tree. "Sorry," he said.

Ahead of them Alan scurried along, as if he were walking on a carpet.

Keeping up with a jungle man was not easy.

At the edge of the forest, where it met the river, Alan finally stopped.

Judy, Peter, and Sarah limped and stumbled toward him.

"Sssshhhhh!" He turned and waved at them urgently in a way that meant *hide yourselves*.

As they ducked into the undergrowth, Alan dropped to his knees.

Just beyond him, on a flat rock that jutted into the river, the pelican stood peacefully. It faced away from them all, sunning itself.

At its feet was the Jumanji board.

Alan crawled silently among the reeds along the riverbank. Emerging on the rock, he crouched low and approached the Jumanji board on tiptoe.

The pelican turned its head toward Alan.

"Easy there, bud," Alan said, reaching for the game. "You have something of mine."

Snnnnap! The pelican lunged forward, nipping Alan's hand with its beak.

"Yyyyeow!" Falling backward onto the rock, Alan massaged his sore hand. "Okay, let's try the barter system."

Alan leaned out over the river. He stared at the current, stock-still, for a long moment.

Then, with one nimble thrust, he reached into the water and pulled out a live, flapping fish.

Judy gasped in amazement.

The pelican perked up. It waddled closer to Alan, opening its mouth hungrily.

"Oh, you like that, do you?" Alan held the fish high, teasing the pelican, drawing it closer to the riverbank.

Then, before the bird could devour it, Alan threw the fish across the rock.

The pelican went after it, flapping its wings.

Its feet splayed out for a split-second, clipping the edge of the Jumanji board.

Alan dived for it. The board teetered for a moment.

Then it fell in.

Judy almost passed out. Sarah sputtered in shock.

Peter sprang to his feet and ran. The current was carrying the game downstream. He followed the river, leaping over rocks.

Racing around a bend, he overtook the game. A few yards ahead, he spotted a tree that had fallen toward the river. It dangled over the water, barely rooted in the ground.

Peter jumped onto it. It creaked, sinking closer to the water.

He cast a glance upstream. The Jumanji board was floating toward him, bobbing on the whitecaps.

This was it. If Peter couldn't get it now, the game was history.

He walked along the branch. With each step, it bounced, throwing him off balance.

Crouching low, arms out, he continued. The branch began to narrow, the wood to feel wetter. Peter's feet slipped. He held his arms out for stability.

The game was rising and sinking, approaching fast.

Peter lined himself up, then reached down. Too far.

The branch was about four feet above the water. He was going to miss it.

Gym class. Parallel bars. The thought popped into his mind. He didn't question it for a moment.

He sat down, locking his knees around the branch. Then he let his upper body fall backward, toward the raging current.

"No, Peter!" he heard Sarah and Judy scream from the riverbank.

The board was coming closer. Inches away. Peter stretched his fingertips.

Too far!

Desperately Peter swung his body. With a deep groan, the branch sagged downward.

The Jumanji board raced directly underneath him.

Peter's fingers touched the edge of the board.

Got it!

He clutched the board tightly and bounced upward. Holding it to his chest, he mounted the branch and walked along it to the bank.

Judy and Sarah were gaping. Behind them, Alan ran up and stopped short.

129

"That was so cool, Peter," Judy remarked.

"Very intense," Sarah agreed.

Peter beamed proudly.

Frowning, Alan cleared his throat. "Nice work," he mumbled grudgingly. "Now, let's get a move on."

As he turned and bounded away, Sarah gave him a sarcastic salute.

The four of them made their way back through the forest, then onto the road that led to town.

They were passing over a cast-iron bridge when Officer Bentley's cruiser roared toward them from a side road. It skidded to a sudden stop, cutting them off.

Bentley barged out of the driver's door and grabbed Alan by the arm. "Wouldn't you know an APB to pursue a stampede of wild animals would lead straight to *you*," he snarled. "Now, where's that trigger-happy guy who was chasing you?"

"I don't know what you're talking about," Alan replied.

"Fine," Bentley snapped. "I'm taking you in for questioning, wiseguy."

"I'm not going anywhere!" Alan said.

Bentley grabbed the handcuffs from his belt and slapped them on Alan's wrists.

"Wait a minute!" Sarah protested. "Please! Uh . . . don't take him away. He's — "

"Her fiancé!" Judy cut in.

Sarah gulped.

"I thought he was your uncle," Bentley said.

"He is!" Judy shot back. "But he's the half-brother of my mother's sister from her father's first marriage."

"Please don't take away our half-uncle," Peter pleaded. "He's the only family we've got."

Phut.

No one heard the silenced rifle but Alan. His eyes darted toward the cruiser as the bullet passed silently overhead.

Van Pelt. He was below the bridge somewhere. Hiding in the bushes.

"It's all right," Alan said to Peter. "I'll be back soon."

Van Pelt was a great shot. A marksman. Alan had to do something. Be a moving target. Keep him from lining up a clear shot.

Alan bobbed to the right and left. He ducked and jumped and twisted, yanking Officer Bentley toward the cruiser. "Let's go, Carl!" he urged.

Bentley looked at Alan as if he'd lost his mind.

Sarah shook her head angrily. "You were the

131

one who said you'd *never* abandon your friends, Alan!"

Phut.

Out of the corner of his eye, Alan saw a bullet strike the dirt behind the cruiser. He leaped into the front seat.

"And now you're just leaving us holding the bag!" Sarah went on.

"A bag's going to be holding *me* if you don't let me get out of here!" Alan called out. "Carl! Come on!"

Bentley folded himself into the driver's seat. As he slammed the door, he said to the others, "I suggest you all get home. Something's not right in Brantford."

He gunned the engine and drove away.

None of them saw Van Pelt stalking through the undergrowth, thirty yards away, cursing under his breath and vowing to kill Alan Parrish.

"He's totally nuts," Judy said to Sarah. "But how are we going to finish the game?"

"We're not," Sarah replied. "I'm not going to play without him."

"Judy!"

Peter's anguished cry gave Judy a start. She looked behind her.

Peter was kneeling over the Jumanji board, staring at the black circle.

"What happened?" Sarah asked.

"I thought I could end the game myself," Peter said. "I was only ten spaces away!"

They all read the message in the circle:

A law of Jumanji having been broken,
You will slip back even more than your token.

"You tried to *cheat?*" Sarah asked.

"I tried to drop the dice so they'd turn up ten!" Peter explained.

Judy noticed that Peter's token had slipped back to the first square.

But that was not the worst part.

"Your hands, Peter!" she cried in horror. "Look at your hands!"

Slowly Peter held them up.

They were sprouting thick, dark fur!

CHAPTER 19

"**M**ale, late fifties, scratching and showing symptoms of jaundice ... owner reports that perps are monkeys ... thirteen customers at supermarket feverish and scratching ... baboon seen in Dumpster behind the diner ..."

The voice crackled over the cruiser's CB radio. Officer Bentley listened intently. "So what's this all about?" he asked. "I *know* you know."

Alan leaned forward in the backseat, resting his cuffed hands on his lap. "I can't explain it to you, Carl. And you wouldn't believe me even if I could."

"Wait a minute, wait a minute! How do you know my name is Carl?"

"I know more than that. You used to work

on the stamping line at Parrish Shoes. They called you the Sole Man."

"Yeah . . . that's right," Bentley said warily. "Until old man Parrish fired me."

"*Fired* you?"

Bentley exhaled heavily. "And I had something that could've put this town on the map."

He fell silent, staring sullenly ahead. Alan examined his face curiously in the rearview mirror.

"I don't know what they wear on their feet where *you've* been," Bentley continued. "But look around here — air-cushioned, leather-sided, high-topped, waffle-soled sneakers! And I saw it all coming, back in nineteen sixty-nine. I made a shoe that put anything they have on the street today to shame!"

Alan thought back. In the recesses of his memory, he recalled the day he'd hidden from Billy Jessup in the shoe factory. He pictured his dad's disapproving face . . . the conversation with Carl . . . it was all filtering in, all except the ending.

"So . . . what happened?" Alan asked.

"The Parrish kid put it on the sole-stamping belt," Bentley replied bitterly. "Wrecked the shoe, wrecked the machine, and got me fired on the spot."

I ran away. The realization hit Alan like a sledgehammer. *I let Carl take the blame.*

"This town turned mean when the factory folded," Bentley went on. "Lucky for me, though, because they had to double the police force from three to six. Otherwise I wouldn't have a job."

"I know it doesn't mean anything," Alan said, "but I apologize."

"Apologize for what?"

"For ruining everything."

Bentley's eyes shot up to the rearview mirror. He scrutinized Alan's features carefully.

Then he let out a sudden, astonished gasp.

SCREEEEEE . . . He hit the brakes and the cruiser slid to a stop.

Bentley spun around to get a closer look. A closer look at the man who had grown from the boy who had stolen his life.

Alan was going to jail. He would need bail money. That much Sarah knew. She agreed to raid her bank account to get him out.

She, Judy, and Peter hitched into town on the back of a pickup truck. Thanking the driver, they climbed out at the Brantford town square.

Around them was utter pandemonium. Screeching and chattering echoed from within buildings. An ambulance raced by. Looters ran from stores through shattered doors and windows, clutching armfuls of merchandise. Boxes flew out of second-story windows, crashing to the sidewalk. Cars were parked on the grass, the sidewalks, and the streets at odd angles. Their doors hung open, some with motors running and radios blaring.

Not far away, a man fell to the sidewalk, scratching and groaning. A motorcycle whizzed by him, driven by three screeching monkeys.

Peter watched them, riveted. *Me, too!* The thought rose up instinctively. He almost dropped the Jumanji board and ran after them. He wanted to hop on for the ride. Be one of them. But he held himself back.

With dread, he glanced down. His arms poked out of his sleeves, at least five inches longer than they used to be. Covered with thick brown hair.

Which was also growing on his face.

As he followed Sarah and Judy to a cash machine, he rocked from side to side, loping. His shoes hurt like crazy. His feet were growing.

Sarah groaned when she saw the message on the ATM screen: TEMPORARILY OUT OF SERVICE.

"Maybe we can bail him out with a check," she mused.

Judy heard heavy footsteps behind them. She turned and let out a scream.

Grinning, Van Pelt pulled the Jumanji board from Peter's hand. "Tell that coward that if he treasures this toy, he can meet me at . . ."

His voice trailed off. He was now looking at the painting on the board. His brow furrowed thickly as he held it up.

The hunter under the game logo glowered back at him.

It was a perfect likeness.

As he stood there, mouth open, a crowd of panicked townspeople rounded a corner. Screaming, scratching, jabbering, they engulfed Van Pelt, sweeping him along.

Peter leaped into their midst, elbowing his way to Van Pelt. He snatched away the board and took off.

Right into the pathway of a careening car.

"*Peter!*" Judy cried out.

Peter jumped out of the way as the car stopped. The driver emerged, livid with anger.

But before the man could utter a word, he froze. His eyes fixed on something over Peter's shoulder.

The ground began to rumble.

Peter didn't have to look. As the driver bolted down the street, Peter jumped into the empty car.

Pounding the blacktop, shoulder to shoulder, the rhinos charged up Main Street. Shrieking, people jumped between buildings and into broken storefronts.

The rhinos headed straight for the car. They trampled everything in their path — trash cans, fire hydrants, street signs — as if they were cardboard.

Peter hunkered down as low as he could. Throwing his long arms over his head, he lay down on the Jumanji board.

With a sudden, thunderous *CRRRRUNCH*, the stampede hit the car.

CHAPTER 20

POW! POW! POW! POW!
Peter could hear the tires popping beneath him. The windows blew outward. The roof caved downward toward him.

He gritted his teeth and closed his eyes. He imagined his obituary: "Half-Baboon, Half-Human Trampled by Rhinos in New England."

What a way to go.

The noise was beyond mere sound. It was like a solid blow to the ears.

CRRRRRRRRUNCCCHH!

Now the elephants had arrived. Peter could hear the difference. The roof sank closer toward him. He was running out of space. He had a sudden empathy for canned tuna fish.

Then he felt cold metal on his back. He cast a frightened glance upward. Battered and pulverized, the roof was trapping him, flattening him into a sheet.

He knew he was screeching because his mouth was open and his throat hurt. But over the stampede, he couldn't hear a thing.

Then, abruptly, it all stopped.

The scream caught in Peter's throat. He saw nothing, heard nothing but the boom of receding hoofbeats. As if it were a dream.

Was this what death was like? Pitch-black, stuffy, quiet?

He opened his eyes. He hadn't realized they were closed.

The car roof was still pressed against his back. He looked out of the smashed window and saw blacktop. Squirming, he pulled the Jumanji board out from underneath him.

He was alive. He could still play.

Maybe death would have been better.

"*Peter!*" Judy's hysterical voice filtered through the wreckage from outside.

An arm reached in. Peter smiled.

Until he realized it was covered with a thick, khaki sleeve.

"Give me that, boy," growled Van Pelt.

"No!" Peter clung to the game. He tried to shove it out of Van Pelt's reach, but there was no room.

Van Pelt easily plucked it through the narrow, crumpled window and ran off.

"Help!" Peter cried. "Get me out of here!"

Judy and Sarah ran to the car. Peter held onto their outstretched hands. Grunting, twisting, he wiggled his way toward the window opening.

As he spilled out onto the street, he looked back in horror at the metal pancake that had been his hiding place.

It had been close. Very close.

But there was no time to think about that. They needed to get the game back.

Judy and Sarah took off down the street, in the direction Van Pelt had gone.

Peter followed them. Hard as he tried; he couldn't run like a normal human. His legs had bowed, and his arms dangled as he loped along.

They leaped over garbage, broken glass, flattened boxes, and crates. Sarah sprinted ahead, disappearing for a moment around a corner. "There!" she shouted.

Peter and Judy pulled up in time to see Van Pelt enter a giant discount store called Sir Sav-a-Lot.

They darted across a parking lot and into the store.

The aisles were in chaos. Looters scavenged. Clerks chased them. Other clerks chased and *then* scavenged. Goods were strewn all over the floor — books, batteries, umbrellas, toys, food.

But no Van Pelt. Judy, Sarah, and Peter scoured the store, one aisle at a time. Household goods, sportswear, health and beauty aids, toys . . .

"Look!" Judy cried out.

At the end of the toy aisle, atop a glass counter, sat the Jumanji box.

"Wait here," Sarah said. She rushed down the aisle and grabbed the box.

Van Pelt shot up from behind the counter and grabbed her wrist.

"I might have known," Sarah muttered.

"But you didn't," Van Pelt gloated. "Now, when Alan hears that I have you, he'll come. And I'll bag him at last!"

"Great plan, genius, but how's he going to find out you've got me?"

Pointing his rifle to the ceiling, he fired off a round of bullets. *"DON'T MOVE, WOMAN!"* he bellowed. *"OR I'LL BLOW YOU TO CHIPS AND SNIPPETS!"*

Plaster cascaded to the floor. Looters dropped their merchandise. In a screaming panic, people ran for the exits.

Van Pelt smiled confidently. "Alan will hear of your predicament soon enough."

Under cover of the next aisle, Judy and Peter approached Van Pelt. Peter sneaked around the counter on all fours — which, with his new shape, was becoming much more comfortable.

Leaping, he bit Van Pelt in the knee.

The hunter yowled with pain, releasing Sarah. Judy ran to the counter, lifted the laser price scanner, and beamed it into his eyes.

Van Pelt shrank backward, covering his eyes with one hand. With his other hand, he sprayed the store with rifle shots.

Sarah took the game board and ran, with Judy and Peter close behind.

CHAPTER 21

Bentley wasn't convinced. Not totally. He bought Alan's identity. The resemblance was there, the memories were accurate.

But the Jumanji stuff? Forget it. Bentley wouldn't hear a word of it.

Frustrated, Alan paced outside the cruiser. His hands were still cuffed together, and he felt like a caged animal. They had been parked by the side of the road, arguing away, while Van Pelt and half the wildlife of Jumanji were running loose.

"Carl, you've got to believe me," Alan pleaded. "If you let me go, I can stop all this. I'll explain later. But right now, you've got to help me!"

Leaning against the driver's-side door, Bentley raised a skeptical eyebrow. "Last time I tried to help you, I lost everything I had."

"It's different this time!" Alan held out his cuffed hands. "Please."

Reluctantly Bentley reached for his keychain. "I know I'm going to regret this," he mumbled, unlocking the cuffs. "Okay, what can I do?"

"Nothing." In one blinding move, Alan snapped one cuff on Bentley's right wrist and the other on the door frame. "This is something I have to do on my own."

Seizing the keys from Bentley's belt, he flung them into a nearby field. Then he bolted up the road.

"AAAALLLLLLLAAAAAAANNNN!" Bentley howled.

"You'll thank me someday!" Alan called out.

Fuming, Bentley struggled with the cuffs. Inside the cruiser, Lorraine's voice blared through his radio: "Carl! Come in, Carl. Possible hostage situation at the Sir Sav-a-Lot, involving a woman, two children, and a heavily armed Caucasian male resembling the perpetrator you referenced earlier. Are you there, Carl?"

Overhearing, Alan ran back to the cruiser. "Van Pelt!" he exclaimed. "He's got them!"

Before Bentley could say a word, Alan began shoving him into the cruiser. "Get in!" Alan urged. "We're going downtown."

"What?" Bentley grunted. "How do you expect me to — " His body was twisted into a knot. His right arm, attached to the door, was crossed over his chest.

Alan stuffed him into the driver's seat and climbed in beside him. "Don't worry, I've done this before," he said, turning the ignition. "Once."

The car roared to life. Scrunched up against Bentley, Alan pulled down the gearshift.

RRRRROMMMMMM! The cruiser jumped away from the curb.

Backward.

Alan and Bentley lurched toward the windshield. Jamming the brake, Alan shifted blindly. The cruiser spun around. When they were pointed toward town, Alan stepped on the gas.

The cruiser sped forward, fishtailing down the road. Bentley cowered against the door.

"Where's this Sir Sav-a-Lot place?" Alan asked.

"Monroe and Elm," Bentley replied.

"Next to the Episcopal church?"

"Church? That's a Speedy Burger now. Or it *was*, but who knows what's left of it now that the folks here have gone out of their minds."

In his rearview mirror, Alan spotted flashing lights. He slowed down as a police motorcycle pulled up beside him.

On it were three grinning monkeys. One of them twirled a revolver.

Bentley gasped.

Shaking his head in disgust, Alan pressed the gas pedal and left the monkeys in the dust.

At the Sir Sav-a-Lot, Sarah ran for her life among the aisles. Holding tight to the Jumanji board, she ducked into the women's-apparel section.

Van Pelt was close behind. Three bullets smacked into a mannequin to Sarah's left. She ducked to the right, down the middle of casual wear.

Judy waved to her urgently from the home-lighting section, a few aisles away. She pointed to a shopping cart just ahead of Sarah.

Grabbing the cart, Sarah tossed in the Jumanji board and pushed.

The cart careened across the store. Judy grabbed it and ran.

Van Pelt barreled after her, snorting and wild-eyed.

In sporting goods, Peter searched desperately for something he could use as a weapon, a booby trap, anything to stop Van Pelt.

He stopped in front of a large aluminum

canoe. An idea took form in his mind. A brilliant, nasty idea.

I may look like Bubbles the chimp, he thought, but I can still think like an eight-year-old boy.

He pulled down the canoe and set it on the floor. Then, as quickly he could, he gathered the rest of the equipment he needed — some rope, a scuba outfit with double air tanks, and a kayak oar.

First he separated the tanks from the gear. Using the rope, he strapped one tank to the canoe's port gunwale, the other to the starboard.

Next he tied the oar onto the canoe, laying it across widthwise, so that the paddles stuck out from each side.

When that was secure, he pointed the bow into the nearest intersection of the aisles.

In the distance he could hear Van Pelt shouting and stomping closer.

Quickly he fetched a hammer and a gallon bottle of liquid detergent from housewares. Unscrewing the top, he spilled the stuff into the intersection in front of the canoe, making a wide puddle.

Finally he covered the canoe with a canvas tarp. Clutching the hammer, he crouched behind the contraption and waited.

Van Pelt barged around a corner and into the middle of the intersection.

Peter pulled off the tarp.

WWHAAAANGGG! WWHAAAANGGG!

He smacked the two nozzles with his hammer.

PPPPPSSSSSSSHHHHHHH . . . Air gushed out from both tanks, propelling the canoe forward.

Toward Van Pelt.

Van Pelt tried to run. His jackboots slipped on the detergent. His legs wobbled beneath him.

The canoe shot between them like a torpedo. With a resounding *thwack,* the kayak paddles clipped him in the knees.

Roaring with pain, Van Pelt toppled forward into the canoe.

It rocketed across the slick floor, into the camping display. A smiling mannequin family, dressed in crisp outdoor clothing, fell onto Van Pelt in a jumble of arms and legs.

The canoe plunged through the open flap of an enormous canvas tent. With a loud rip, the tent collapsed.

There the canoe finally stopped, under a pile of backpacks, stoves, canvas, and plastic body parts.

From within the mess came furious shouting and wild gunfire.

Around a corner raced Sarah. Judy was close behind, carrying the Jumanji box.

"Come on, Peter!" Sarah shouted. "Let's get out of here!"

The three of them ran for the door.

Behind them, Van Pelt clawed his way out of the heap. He clenched his teeth against the excruciating pain in his legs.

Spotting the three escapees, though, he stood up straight and alert.

The pain was forgotten. They were easy targets.

He raised his rifle and took aim.

CHAPTER 22

At Monroe and Elm, Alan yanked the steering wheel to the left.

Sir Sav-a-Lot loomed large through the shattered windshield. The cruiser flew toward it at seventy miles an hour.

"Slow down!" Officer Bentley commanded.

Alan stomped on the brake.

The pedal sank to the floor. Yellowish fluid spurted out the side of the cruiser.

Alan pumped again. And again.

Nothing. The brakes were dead.

As the cruiser hurtled toward the solid wall of Sir Sav-a-Lot, Alan and Bentley exchanged a final word:

"*WAAAAAAAAAAAAHHHHHH!*"

Inside the store, Van Pelt chortled. The three weaklings were heading for the side exit. They thought they could outwit him.

He calmly pulled the trigger.

Phhhut!

The bullet screamed through the air. Van Pelt lowered the rifle and smiled.

Bull's-eye!

The bullet smashed the latch on a rack of RV tires, directly over the side exit.

The rack swung away from the wall. Tires cascaded downward. Sarah and Judy stopped short, blocked by the avalanche.

They watched in horror as Peter was buried under a mountain of black rubber.

As they yanked tires away, trying to free Peter, Van Pelt sauntered toward them. Sarah shrank away, holding the Jumanji board to her chest.

"Stop your cringing," Van Pelt snarled. "It's unsportsmanlike to shoot defenseless women."

Sarah bristled. "That is absolutely the sickest thing I have ever heard!"

With a raucous laugh, Van Pelt grabbed the Jumanji board from her. "He will come to me now!"

BOOOOOOOOOOOM!

The noise behind Van Pelt was like a cannon shot. He turned to look. Several aisles away, merchandise was flying into the air. He could hear the growl of an engine, a series of crashes . . .

He took a step backward, toward the house-paint display. From that perspective, he spotted the hole in the far wall.

Just then a display rack exploded in front of him — and Officer Bentley's cruiser came barreling through.

Van Pelt had faced a lion close enough to smell its breath. He had stared down a rhinoceros without flinching. Wild animals were nothing for a hunter like him.

But this — *this* was real terror.

He jumped away. The Jumanji board flew from his hand.

With a bone-jarring crash, the cruiser plowed into a stack of paint cans. Van Pelt fell to the floor, covering his head, as cans burst and toppled all around him.

Against the wall, a heap of twisted metal, the cruiser finally died.

Alan jumped out and ran to Judy and Sarah.

Officer Bentley staggered out after him, weak-kneed and bewildered. His handcuff yanked the driver's-side door, which fell off with a dull clank.

He glanced at Alan. He looked at his cuffs. Then, in a daze, he trudged away, dragging the door after him.

"Thank goodness you're all right!" Alan said to Judy and Sarah. "Where's Peter?"

Sarah pointed a shaky finger to the mound of tires.

Alan raced over, yanking the tires away. Soon Peter's face appeared.

Or what had been Peter's face. Covered with hair, jaw jutting forward, it looked more and more like a baboon's.

Alan couldn't help but gasp. He didn't know what had happened, but he suspected it had to do with the game.

There was no time to waste. If they didn't finish playing soon, Peter was going to wind up in a zoo.

CHAPTER 23

Driving on the outskirts of town, Aunt Nora listened intently to a soothing voice on a cassette tape:

"So remember, circumstances are never out of our control." A soft beep sounded. "End of tape three. Please insert tape number four, 'The Three C's: Composure, Charisma, and Clooooobaaarrchrizzzz —'"

The tape groaned to a halt.

"Oh, great," Aunt Nora muttered.

She braked to a stop at a red light. When she ejected the tape, the radio came on:

"Now for an update on the extraordinary events unfolding in Brantford, New Hampshire," the announcer intoned, "where at least ninety-eight people have been hospitalized with symptoms ranging from inexplicable fevers and rashes to violent seizures. Local resources have been strained to breaking point, and state officials are now asking anyone experiencing such symptoms to dial a special hotline number, 1-800-555-RASH. Immunologists from Atlanta's Centers for Disease Control have stated that . . ."

"Oh, no," Aunt Nora whispered to herself. "The kids!"

The ground began to shake. Aunt Nora looked around curiously. How odd. Did New England have earthquakes?

As the light changed, she started to take her foot off the brake.

But she jammed it back down again. The intersection was suddenly blocked.

By rhinoceroses. Charging from left to right. Snorting and unfriendly-looking.

Her jaw dropped.

What was on that tape? It had completely affected her brain.

Opening her car door, she stepped out. The dust from the stampede billowed around her.

Focused ahead, she didn't notice the monkey jumping away from the stampede, hiding in her car.

She watched as the elephants and zebras charged by. Then, numbly, she plopped herself back into the car and shifted into gear.

The intersection was now rutted and filled

with debris. Aunt Nora steered through it slowly, then picked up speed on the other side.

From the backseat leaped the monkey. He landed next to her with an admiring grin.

"YEEEEEAAAHHHH!"

Aunt Nora slammed on the brakes. The car jumped off the road and into a ditch.

Screaming, she pushed her way out the door and scrambled to the street.

As she ran off, the monkey poked its head out the passenger window and scolded her angrily.

It was a long way from the Sir Sav-a-Lot to Jefferson Street, but Alan, Sarah, Judy, and Peter made it in no time.

Just outside the Parrish house, Peter began whimpering. His body was gnarled and stooped, and he seemed to have trouble walking.

Looking at him, Sarah's eyes moistened. "Talk to him, Alan," she whispered.

Alan felt for the poor little guy. This transformation must have been tough. Approaching Peter stiffly, Alan tried to imagine the right words to say. In all those years in the jungle, he never *had* to give advice.

"Well, Peter," Alan began, clearing his

throat, "you cheated, and now you're going to have to face the consequences like a man."

"Ohhhhhhhhhhh!" Peter groaned.

"Come on, chin up," Alan continued. "Crying never did anybody any good. If you've got a problem, you've got to face it."

Peter burst out crying.

Terrific, Alan thought to himself. The kid's a monkey, and I'm telling him to look on the bright side. "You're right, Peter, you're right. I'm totally insensitive. Twenty-six years buried in the darkest, remotest jungle, and I *still* became my father!" He threw his arms around the sobbing monkey-boy. "I'm sorry, Peter."

Whew. Alan felt relieved he figured that one out.

"It's not that," Peter said weakly.

Alan pulled back. "Then what is it?"

"Look down," Peter said, red-faced.

Alan saw a tuft of brown fur sticking out the bottom of Peter's pant leg. Quickly he turned Peter around and ripped a hole in the seat of his pants.

He reached in and pulled out a long tail.

Sarah and Judy were white with shock.

Peter smiled with relief. "Thanks."

"Okay, now, don't worry," Alan said, walking up the porch steps with Peter. "We'll get you turned back to you in no time flat. We're going right back in there, sitting down, and together we'll finish this thing, no matter — "

He pushed open the front door, and the words caught in his throat.

"*Whaaaat?*" he said in a horrified whisper.

Behind him, Sarah gasped. "Oh, no!"

The foyer walls were a deep, lush green, teeming with thick vines. Dappled light from the chandelier shone through the leaves.

The ceiling, floors, stairs, furniture — the vines had wrapped around everything. The house was being swallowed by a growing jungle.

"Maybe we should play somewhere else," Sarah suggested.

"No, I've been dealing with this stuff all my life," Alan said, marching inside. He pointed back over his shoulder. "It's the stuff out there that throws me."

Zzzzz . . . zzzz . . . zzzz . . .

In the hardware section of the Sir Sav-a-Lot, Officer Bentley used a hacksaw to cut through the handcuff chain.

With a clank, the police cruiser door fell to the floor. Bentley flexed his arm.

He was finally free.

Bentley raced over to the automotive section. Among the debris-strewn shelves, he found a can of brake fluid. Quickly he ran over to his cruiser.

Sweeping away all the paint cans, he opened the hood. Then he emptied the fluid into its case and slammed the hood back down.

It slid off and crashed to the floor.

There was no time to worry about that. Bentley jumped into the driver's seat and started the engine.

The cruiser roared to life. He backed it slowly away from the fallen hood, then stepped on the brake.

The car stopped. The brakes were working!

Yanking the steering wheel to the left, he weaved among the wreckage, heading for the exit.

"Lorraine, this is Carl!" he called into his CB mike. "I know who's behind all this insanity. I'm on my way to the Parrish house. Give me some backup . . . Lorraine?"

"*EEEEE-ee-ee-oo-oo-aaaaaaah!*" came the response.

The station sounded like a monkey house. Bentley threw down the mike in disgust and stepped on the gas.

As he drove out of the store, a hand reached out from the pile of paint cans. Slowly Van Pelt clawed his way out. He was dazed and half-conscious.

And he was very, very angry.

CHAPTER 24

"**H**elp! Help!" Aunt Nora waved her arms at the approaching car. "Stop!"

Finally. She'd been running forever without seeing a single vehicle.

And what a vehicle. A police cruiser that looked like it had been through a food processor — dented and scratched, no driver's door, and no hood.

Not to mention the paint splotches all over it.

Officer Bentley pulled to a stop. "You all right, ma'am?" he asked.

"No, I am not all right!" Aunt Nora replied. "I need to get home immediately."

"Where do you live?"

"Jefferson Street. The old Parrish place."

Bentley did a double take. "Do you have kids? A boy and a girl?"

"Oh, no." Aunt Nora blanched. "What happened?"

"I'll tell you on the way. Get in."

"I knew it! I knew I couldn't handle this! I'm a terrible mother — and now something terrible has happened!"

Through the window behind Bentley a vine tendril snaked in, reaching toward him.

Aunt Nora tried to say something, but the words tangled in her throat.

Instead, she just screamed.

"Calm down, ma'am," Bentley said in his best police-officer-in-charge voice. "You're overreacting."

Aunt Nora pointed to the vine, which was now inching toward his neck.

Officer Bentley turned around. "Aaaa-agghhh!"

He dived out the door.

The vine shot across his empty seat. Then it continued, wrapping around the bottom of the cruiser.

With a deep, gravelly scraping sound, the cruiser slid sideways. The vine pulled it into a thick bush, where it vanished from sight.

"Fine!" Bentley bellowed. "Take it!"

Turning to Aunt Nora, he said coolly, "Sorry, ma'am, we'll have to walk."

Alan stepped into the plant-covered parlor. He kicked aside some vines on the floor and set down the Jumanji board.

"Well," he said with a shrug, "this place always needed a little more life."

Sarah, Judy, and Peter kneeled by the board. As Alan sat, he caught Sarah's glance.

For the first time, he felt no anger at her, no bitterness. For two and a half decades they'd existed totally apart, not even thinking of one another. But in a sense, their lives couldn't be complete . . . until now.

As Sarah picked up the dice, Alan wanted to tell her what he was feeling, tell her now before something else awful happened.

But the look on her face told him he didn't have to. She knew, too. They were in this as a team.

"Sarah," Judy said, "if you roll a twelve, you'll win!"

Sarah closed her eyes. She shook the dice, murmuring a wish under her breath. Then she rolled.

Four . . . and one. *Five.*

To a chorus of disappointed sighs, the dice moved.

" 'Every month at the quarter moon,' " Sarah read, " 'there is a monsoon in your lagoon.' *Lagoon?* Good thing we're inside." She handed Judy the dice. "Judy, quick. It's your turn."

CRRRRRRACK!

Lightning flashed through the house.

The floor rumbled. Judy sprang to her feet, remembering the stampede.

But no animals came this time. Only rain.

Lots of rain.

Curtains of rain. Rain that fell so violently, they could barely see each other.

Instantly the parlor was flooded. The game board floated away.

Alan grabbed it. Around him the water rose to ankle level . . . knee level . . .

"What do we do now?" Sarah shouted over the noise.

"Get to higher ground!" Alan shouted back.

Shielding their faces against the torrential downpour, the four players fought their way into the foyer.

Water cascaded down the stairs like a

mighty river. They tried to climb upward, but the current pushed them back.

Now Judy and Peter had to tread. The water was rising toward the ceiling.

Alan began swimming toward the chandelier, which dangled close to the water's surface. *"Come on!"* he urged.

But Sarah was flailing wildly, in a blind panic.

"Alaaaaaaan!" she cried.

Behind her, teeth jutting from their grinning jaws, were two giant crocodiles!

CHAPTER 25

"**S**wim!" Alan shouted.

He led the way to the chandelier. Under it, the dining room table was floating by. Alan hoisted himself on it. He set the game board down, then reached to help up Sarah, Judy, and Peter.

Snnnnnap! Jaws clamped together so close to Judy she could feel the breeze.

She screamed and leaped away.

Snnnnnap! Snnnnnap! The crocs attacked them from both sides.

Directly beneath the chandelier, Alan cupped his hands. "Climb!"

Judy scooped up the game board. She stepped into his hands, grabbed onto the huge chandelier, and pulled herself up.

Next Peter scrambled up with monkeylike agility.

With a dull *whump*, a crocodile flopped onto the table. Alan and Sarah seesawed upward. They smashed headlong into the chandelier.

Peter lost his hold. Windmilling his long arms, he fell into the flood.

"Hellllllp!" he shrieked.

Rising out of the water, one of the crocs opened his mouth around Peter's head.

Alan knelt down. He grabbed Peter's tail and pulled.

Snnnnnap! The mouth closed. Peter flew up to the chandelier in one piece.

But Sarah was sliding — right into the waiting jaws of the other croc. "Alaaaaan!" she cried.

Her left foot landed on the croc's bottom jaw. Her right landed on the top. She froze.

The croc opened and shut his mouth, eager to eat.

Sarah's legs scissored in and out with the motion. "*AAAAAAGGGGHHH!*" she wailed.

Alan dived onto the animal. He wrestled it back into the water.

As he disappeared under, fighting, Sarah clutched onto the chandelier and pulled herself up.

She, Peter, and Judy watched, rigid with fear. In the roiling water, they could only see a flash of skin, a ripple of green leather.

The other croc paddled closer, eager to share the upcoming meal.

Aunt Nora and Officer Bentley plodded up the walkway to the house. As they came nearer, they heard screaming from within. And a noise like a running shower.

Looking down, Aunt Nora noticed water streaming under the door. "Oh, no!" she gasped. "*Oh, no!* Those poor children."

Bentley drew his revolver with one hand and clenched the door knob with the other. "Let me handle this, ma'am."

With a strong yank, he opened the door.
FOOOOOOSH!

It flew off its hinges. Rising up from below. Smacking into Bentley and Aunt Nora, lifting them upward.

They shot out toward the street, on the crest of a tidal wave. Furniture and broken vines tumbled around them in the water.

Clutching onto the door for dear life, they surfed over the front lawn and down Jefferson Street.

Which, at the moment, looked more like Jefferson Rapids.

Inside the house, Judy, Peter, and Sarah watched the water empty out the doorway. It was as if a plug had been pulled from a giant bathtub.

Below them, the current pulled Alan and the crocodiles toward the door. Alan paddled ferociously for the chandelier.

Peter reached his long arm down. Alan grabbed his hand, pulling hard.

The chandelier swung. Peter struggled to hold on, against the strength of the current and Alan's grip.

His feet slipped off.

Judy lunged after him. As she grabbed onto his ankles, she was pulled off, too.

Sarah held onto Judy. The three of them were now a human chain, stretched from the chandelier to Alan, desperately keeping him from the crocodiles' jaws.

The water level sank fast. The crocs thrashed wildly, snapping at Alan's feet.

On the chandelier, Sarah gave one final tug. The chain jerked forward a fraction of an inch.

In a final powerful flush, the crocodiles were sucked out the door.

Alan held on. Soon his feet felt the floor beneath him. Letting go of Peter, he stood up.

The dining-room table was next to him. He climbed onto it and pulled down Peter, then Judy.

Sarah slid into his arms. As they stepped to the floor, she beamed at him with gratitude and admiration. "You wrestled an alligator for me."

Alan blushed. "It was a crocodile, actually. Alligators don't have that fringe on their hind legs." He averted his eyes from Sarah's loving gaze. "Come on, we'd better get upstairs."

As he bounded upstairs, Sarah shook her head. "Fear of intimacy," she whispered to Judy and Peter.

They caught up to him in the second-floor hallway. To his right, the lion was growling in Aunt Nora's bedroom behind the closed door. To his left, a giant pod blocked passage.

"Upstairs!" Alan declared. "The attic's safer."

They took the spiral stairs two at a time.

The attic was dry, and free of vines. Alan dusted off an old steamer trunk and set the game board on it. Sarah, Judy, and Peter slumped onto boxes and crates, exhausted.

Alan started to roll the dice, then stopped. "*Uh-oh!*" he suddenly cried.

Judy nearly jumped off her crate.

"Did I forget to collect two hundred dollars last time I passed Go?" Alan asked.

As he chuckled at his own joke, the others glared at him.

"Okay, okay." Alan spilled the dice onto the

board. His token moved, and everyone looked at the message:

You better watch just where you stand;
The floor is quicker than quicksand.

Alan sank downward.

Sarah snatched up the dice, Peter the game board. They all jumped away from the steamer trunk.

Except Alan. He was stuck. Beneath him, the floor had become brown, bubbling liquid. It churned and rippled, swallowing him.

"Help me!" Alan shouted desperately, as his feet disappeared below the floor.

CHAPTER 26

"**A**lan, don't struggle!" Sarah urged. Judy stumbled against a music stand. She picked it up and held it out to Alan.

He pulled — but the stand was in two telescoping pieces, and his slid right out of Judy's.

"AAAAAAGGGH!" The floor was up to Alan's chest.

Peter brought over an old trombone. He and Sarah grabbed the mouthpiece and extended the slide to Alan.

"Pull!" Sarah yelled.

Alan did. The slide slid out, and he sank deeper.

"*Stop giving me things that come apart!*" he howled.

Sarah grabbed a wooden chair. Leaning forward, gritting her teeth, she reached out.

Snnap! The moment he took the leg, the chair split along a termite-eaten spot.

Alan was almost under. Sarah dived toward him, reaching with her arms. She fell into the quicksand, elbows first.

Behind them, Judy was struck with a desperate idea.

It was her turn. Maybe her consequence would fix this one. She frantically picked up the dice and rolled.

There is one thing you will learn:
Sometimes you must go back a turn!

Judy's token shot backward on the board.

SHLOOP! The floor instantly became solid.

Alan was trapped. His face, tilted upward, showed above the floor, as did his arms and hands. Next to him, Sarah was on her knees, her forearms locked under the wooden boards.

"Thank you, Judy," Alan said with forced calmness. "That was quick thinking. Sarah and I would like to get out of the floor now. I believe it's Peter's turn."

As Judy and Peter brought the game over, Alan and Sarah turned to each other. They were practically eye to eye, breathing on each other, unable to move from their bizarre positions.

Sarah burst out giggling. "In my support

group, they'd say we were violating each other's personal space."

"Is that bad?" Alan asked.

"Oh, yeah, it's a cardinal sin." Sarah smiled. "But I'm kind of enjoying it, actually."

Alan wanted to look away, but he couldn't. Instead, he forced himself to say exactly what was on his mind. "Me, too."

Ugh, Peter thought. Mush.

He hopped to the Jumanji board and rolled his dice. Together he and Judy read the message:

Need a hand? Why, just you wait.

We'll help you out; we each have eight!

A sudden scuttling noise made them both look up.

Down from the rafters, on a silky thread, dropped a spider the size of a pit bull!

CHAPTER 27

Peter yowled with terror.

Around him, giant spiders dropped like hailstones. Dozens of them — over the game, in the corners, in front of the mirror, by the piano. They hung suspended, waggling their spindly legs, clacking their sharp mouths open and shut.

"What is it?" Alan asked. "I can't see!"

His eyes darted toward the mirror. He let out a bloodcurdling shriek.

Judy picked up the broken music stand and began swatting the spiders left and right.

"Peter!" Alan shouted. "My dad kept an ax in the woodshed. Get it!"

Peter sprinted downstairs and out of the house. He ran to the woodshed, but it was locked.

Grabbing a rusty ax that lay against the side wall, he began striking the lock hard.

Duh.

Ax in hand, he sped back toward the house.

Wet and tired, Aunt Nora entered the house. Her bed-and-breakfast, the dream of her life, was a weed-strangled, rubble-strewn mess.

As she walked through the destroyed lower floor, her heart beat like a jackhammer. "Judy?" she called. "Peter? Kids?"

The distant cry of a jungle bird answered her.

Climbing the stairs, she cast her eyes to the heavens. "If you let them be okay," she murmured, "I'll never let them out of my — "

At the second-floor landing, she stopped in her tracks. Above her, a man's legs and a woman's hands dangled from the ceiling.

She shrieked, backing down the hallway to her bedroom. Groping behind her for the knob, she pushed the door open and ran in.

A lion was stretched across her bed, dozing. Its eyes flickered open. Slowly it raised its head.

Then, baring its teeth, it roared.

Aunt Nora bolted out of the room, slamming the door behind her.

Peter, now almost completely a baboon, came bounding up the stairs with the ax.

"Aunt! Me! Peter!" he screeched, his voice high-pitched and monkeylike.

"YEEEEEEEEAAAAGHHH!" Aunt Nora backed across the hall, right into the linen closet.

"Can't talk now!" Peter cried. "Explain later!"

He slammed the linen-closet door and locked it, turning the key that was in the hole.

Then he ran for the attic stairs.

In the attic, Judy was still smacking spiders. But for each one she batted away, another two approached.

"Sarah!" Alan called out. "It's your turn! All you need is a seven!"

Sarah tried in vain to pull her arms out of the wood. "What am I supposed to do? I can't roll!"

"Wait," Alan said. "Maybe you can!" He looked at her, baring his teeth.

Sarah got the message. "Of course!"

"Judy!" Alan shouted. "Bring the game, quick!"

Judy picked up the game board from the floor. As she ran to Alan, a purple flower sprang up between the floorboards. Its petals opened, revealing poison barbs that dangled like knives.

At that moment, Peter stepped into the attic. He spotted his sister, and then the flower.

"Juuudyyy!" he screamed.

The flower flung itself forward. Barbs shot toward Judy and stuck silently in the back of her neck.

Peter swung his ax and sheared the stem in two. The purple bud went flying.

He raced to his sister. "Judy? You okay?"

"I'm fine!" Judy said, brushing off the barbs. "Help Alan and Sarah!"

She ran to them with the Jumanji board.

"Give me the dice," Sarah said, "in my mouth!"

Judy placed the dice between Sarah's teeth. Sarah clamped down, then let the dice fall to the board. "I can't see it," she cried. "Read the rhyme."

" 'You're almost there, with much at stake,' " Judy read. " 'But now the ground begins to quake.' "

Before the words could sink in, a spider swung toward her.

Then another, and another. They were uniting now, dropping to the floor, scuttling in on Judy as she rose to defend herself.

Then, without warning, they stopped. One

180

by one, they turned tail, scrambling into the corners of the attic.

"All riiiiight!" Peter said.

But his relief was short-lived. A rattling sound was beginning. The furniture vibrated.

Judy collapsed onto the floor, her face bone-white. Peter rushed to her. He lifted her head, cradling it in his lap.

"She was stung by a flower!" he cried out. "What's going to happen to her?"

Alan swallowed hard. "We've got to end the game. It's her only chance."

The floor began to shake — not with the steady rhythm of the stampede, but with an uneven, violent lurching. From below them came a rumble that made Peter's bones shake.

He held his sister tightly. "You're going to be okay, Judy," he whispered. "Does it hurt?"

"No," Judy rasped.

"Liar."

Judy struggled to focus her eyes on Peter. "I wish Mom and Dad were here."

CRRRRRRRACKKK!

Like a wooden zipper, the attic floor split open. Alan dropped straight down, freed from his trap but flailing.

Sarah grabbed his wrists and held tight. Alan swung out over the second floor.

Below him the crack was growing, splitting the entire house, roof to foundation. Opening a black hole in the earth.

All around, plaster fell in chunks from the walls, water spurted from bursting pipes, wires sparked, and furniture slid.

The Jumanji board teetered on the edge of the crevice. The dice fell over, and Alan shook one hand loose to catch them.

"Grab the game!" Alan yelled, stuffing the dice in his pocket.

"I won't let you go!" Sarah insisted.

Another jolt shook the house, as if it had been hit by a giant bowling ball.

The Jumanji board toppled over the edge. With a sharp smack, it landed on the second floor.

It was now perched above a split plank of wood. Below it was nothing but blackness.

Alan broke free of Sarah's grip. He grabbed a hanging vine and jumped.

The vine carried him across the second floor. There he switched to another vine and swung down through the crack, snatching the Jumanji board.

He landed in the living room, panting for breath. His eyes were crossing from exhaustion, his brow dripping with sweat.

But he had the game. And now it was his turn.

He set the game on the floor, behind a thick tangle of vines, then dug his hands into his pocket and pulled out the dice.

His token was five spaces away from the goal. Just five.

"I'm going to do it!" he said to himself. "I'm going to end this game once and for all!"

He shook the dice, positioning his hand over the board.

"Drop it!"

The blood froze in Alan's veins.

He looked toward the front foyer, directly into the barrel of Van Pelt's rifle!

CHAPTER 28

Van Pelt's khakis were ripped and splattered with paint. His pith helmet was dented. His jackboots were scuffed and torn. His handlebar mustache drooped.

But he was the scariest sight Alan had seen in his life.

Slowly Van Pelt stalked Alan, his rifle aimed. "Shouldn't you be running?"

"Not right now," Alan replied. "I've got more important things to do."

"Is this some kind of trick?" Van Pelt narrowed his eyes suspiciously. "What's that in your hand?"

"Nothing."

"Nothing? Then drop it."

Sarah was creeping slowly down the staircase. "You'd better do what he says," she called out cautiously.

Alan squeezed the dice. *Five . . . five . . . five . . .* he wished.

He opened his hand. The dice tumbled.

The first one clattered to the board. It stopped on a three.

The other one kept rolling, right to the edge. . . .

As it fell into the gaping blackness, Alan's heart nearly jumped out of his mouth.

"'More important things to do?'" Van Pelt mocked him. "Like play with toys? Playtime is over, little boy. Run!"

Alan shook his head stubbornly, hoping against all reason. Droplets of sweat fell from his brow, stinging his eyes. He could hear the die clattering inside the crevice, from ledge to ledge among the underground rocks, falling deeper and deeper.

"But you *have* to run!" Van Pelt thundered. "Here, I will let you run until I count three. One . . ."

Van Pelt's finger closed around the trigger. "Two . . ."

The clattering had stopped. The die must have landed. But what number was up?

"And . . . *three!*"

Alan stopped breathing. This was it. Now he'd never be able to make up for all the terrible things he'd done. He'd ruined the lives of every-

one he ever loved and disappeared for years —
and now he'd returned to destroy the house he'd
lived in, the town, maybe the world. What a way
to go.

Van Pelt slowly lowered his rifle. "At last
you have proven yourself."

A sigh of relief burst from Alan. He was
going to be spared!

Not.

"You're worthy quarry," Van Pelt said, rais-
ing his rifle once again.

Out of the corner of his eye, Alan spotted
movement on the Jumanji board. He glanced
down.

The other die must have landed. His token
was sliding forward.

Three spaces . . . four . . .

Five.

Alan swallowed. He looked up at Van Pelt,
his eyes wide with disbelief.

"Any last words?" Van Pelt growled.

Alan could barely get a sound out.
"Jumanji?"

Van Pelt squeezed the trigger.

BLAAAAMMM!

"Noooooooo!" Sarah threw herself across
the room, directly into the path of the flying bullet!

CHAPTER 29

G one.
    The bullet was gone. Into thin air, inches, *millimeters* from Sarah's chest.

She rose to her feet and clutched Alan. He held her tightly.

An eerie quiet settled over the house. The rumbling had stopped.

Alan glanced at Van Pelt. The hunter's fearsome, rock-hard scowl had transformed.

To utter panic.

He was levitating off the ground, spinning. His rifle flew from his hand and vanished. His body began to shimmer, become transparent.

Around them all, the house began to spin . . . and spin . . . until the walls became a blank, and the blank was suddenly filled with the world of Jumanji — the mosquitoes and monkeys and rhinos and elephants and zebras and pelicans and crocodiles and spiders, all circling, tumbling, picking up speed until everything whirled like a cyclone.

Then it all began to narrow at the bottom, into a tail, teeming with wildlife, pointing toward the game board. Toward the center of the black circle.

Weightless and shrinking, it all was sucked inward — animals, vines, and plants, like matter into a black hole.

Last of all, wailing at the top of his lungs, was Van Pelt.

Before Alan and Sarah's eyes, the game they'd begun so long ago finally ended.

PART FOUR

NEW HAMPSHIRE, 1969

CHAPTER 30

GONNNNG! GONNNNG!

Weird. Something must have happened to the grandfather clock, Alan thought. It was working again.

The last time he'd heard it was in 1969, just before he had disappeared.

He squeezed Sarah's arms. What happened to them? They felt so . . . short.

Alan glanced up to her face.

He nearly passed out.

She was thirteen again. Exactly the way he'd remembered her that horrible day the grandfather clock had chimed and he'd . . .

But had he?

He looked at his own arms. A twelve-year-old's, spindly and bare.

And the house — it was beautiful! No vines, no stampede or flood damage. And no dust.

Every piece of furniture was polished and in its place.

Between himself and Sarah, the Jumanji board lay open on a coffee table.

The front door flew open. Alan almost jumped to the ceiling. Sarah recoiled against the couch.

In walked a ghost.

For a dead man, Alan's dad looked pretty good. Robust, even. Not a day older than the last time Alan had seen him.

Which was twenty-six years ago.

Which was now.

Alan rose to his feet. His eyes filled with tears. His throat was so choked with happiness, he could barely speak. "Dad . . . you're *back*."

"I forgot my speech notes," Mr. Parrish replied.

He walked stiffly toward the dining room. Alan recognized that walk. His dad was angry about something. What on earth was it?

Who cared?

During his time in Jumanji, Alan had replayed his life many times. If only he could have done it over again, he'd thought, so many things would be different. So many chances would never be wasted.

Well, now he was back again. Back at the beginning. And he wasn't going to make the same mistakes twice.

He ran across the room and threw his arms around his dad. "Dad, Dad . . . I'm so glad you're back!"

Mr. Parrish flinched. He gave his son a bewildered look. Then, slowly, a shy smile grew across his face. "I've only been gone five minutes."

"It seemed like a lot longer to me," Alan said, wiping away a tear.

His dad chuckled and squeezed Alan tighter. "Hey, I thought you weren't ever talking to me again."

"Whatever I said, I'm sorry."

"Look, Alan, I was angry. I'm . . . I'm sorry, too." He took a deep breath. "And about Cliffside Academy . . ."

"Cliffside?" The ugly memory elbowed its way back into Alan's brain.

"Right. Why don't we talk it over tomorrow, man to man?"

"How about father to son?"

Mr. Parrish smiled warmly and nodded. "Hey, I've got to get going! I'm the guest of honor."

"Dad?" Alan quickly said. "Back in nineteen six — I mean, *today* — in the factory? It wasn't Carl Bentley's fault. *I* put the shoe on the assembly line."

"I'm glad you told me that, son." At that moment, Alan saw an expression on his dad's face that he'd never remembered seeing. One of trust. Pride.

Love.

" 'Bye, Dad," Alan said.

Mr. Parrish turned and left the house.

As the front door shut, Alan felt like dancing. Screaming with joy.

Until he caught sight of the Jumanji board.

"Holy smokes!" he cried out. "Judy and Peter! We have to get up to the attic!"

He started to run, but Sarah calmly held him back. "Alan, they're not there. We're back in nineteen sixty-nine. They don't even exist yet."

Sarah held out her left hand. In it were two tokens. Ones that hadn't been played yet. Judy's and Peter's.

As Alan glanced at the tokens, a distant glint caught his attention. A mirror.

His own reflection took his breath away. Gone were the beard, the animal skins, the broad shoulders and thick arm muscles — and about twelve inches of height.

Seeing himself as twelve-year-old Alan Parrish was a shock.

But he had never been happier in his life.

Minutes later, with Sarah sitting behind him on the long bike seat, Alan pedaled furiously through the dark Brantford streets.

He braked to a stop on the bridge that overlooked the river. The place where Van Pelt had taken potshots at him while he was being handcuffed.

No, Alan thought. It had not happened yet.

And it would *never* happen. He and Sarah were going to make sure of that.

Dismounting from the bike, Sarah held up a large brown grocery bag. Alan reached in and pulled out the Jumanji box, which they had tied up with strong twine. From the twine hung two enormous rocks.

With a grunt, Alan heaved the load over the bridge railing. In the dim moonlight, he and Sarah watched it plunge into the water.

Gone. Forever.

Alan exhaled.

"I'm starting to forget what it's like to be a grown-up," Sarah said.

"Me, too," Alan replied. "That's okay, as long as we don't forget each other."

195

"Or Peter and Judy . . ."

They watched the flowing current, lost in private thoughts. Then Sarah turned and looked into Alan's eyes. "Alan? There's something I've really been wanting to do . . . and I'd better do it before I feel *too* much like a kid."

She wrapped her arms around him. They shared a long, silent kiss, as the world of Jumanji floated away.

PART FIVE

NEW HAMPSHIRE, 1995

CHAPTER 31

Snow fell early in Brantford this winter. It blanketed the prosperous town, quieting the traffic noise, drawing families into the town square for sledding.

Cross-country skiers whizzed past the Parrish Shoe Factory and Annex. The parking lot, usually crowded, lay empty under a coating of white. Over its entrance, a sign bragged PARRISH SHOES: FIVE GENERATIONS OF QUALITY.

Inside, just a few people remained. One of them was the owner and CEO.

Alan Parrish.

He walked down the carpeted hallway that overlooked the factory floor, side by side with his accountant, Marty Lawrence.

"The retailers are furious that you're planning to give away all those shoes again this Christmas," Marty argued.

"Marty," Alan said patiently, "the kids I've given these shoes to aren't going to go out and buy ninety-dollar sneakers, anyway. It's not like anyone's going to lose business."

Marty shook his head. "Yeah, except us."

"Look at it like this: When these kids grow up and get jobs, they'll remember Parrish Shoes and become loyal customers."

As they approached an open door, Carl Bentley stepped out. With gray-flecked hair and a trim European suit over his broad frame, Mr. Bentley was an easy man to respect, and Alan knew it.

"It's an investment in our future," Mr. Bentley said, as if he'd overheard the conversation. With a winning smile, he put his arm around Marty's shoulders. "So why don't you just come in and we'll work out the details?"

As they stepped into the room, Alan shut the door behind them. For a moment, he watched the two silhouettes through the frosted glass above the gold-printed words CARL BENTLEY — PRESIDENT.

He knew Marty would be persuaded. Alan was a pushover, but nobody said no to the inventor of Bentley Air running shoes.

Alan checked his watch. Sarah would be home from her job by now. She was handling her pregnancy well, but it wouldn't be fair to leave her with all the preparations for tonight's Christmas party.

Especially considering how nervous they both were. About the new guests.

Alan took a deep breath. Nervous? Nahhh.

Petrified.

At six-thirty the first guests arrived at the big house on Jefferson Street. Alan greeted them, then ran up and put on his Santa outfit.

As he raced downstairs, the phone rang. Alan ducked into the kitchen and answered. As he spoke, people bustled in and out, taking heaping trays of food from the counters.

"Hello? . . ." Alan said. "Oh, hi, Dad! Yeah, just terrific. . . . The hiking boot line's been doing really great. . . . Yeah, it's been an incredible year. . . . Thanks."

Sarah poked her head into the kitchen. "They're here, hon," she said.

Alan's heart began to race. "I have to run, Dad, my new marketing director just showed up. Give Mom my love. . . . I'll pick you up at the airport Christmas Eve. . . . 'Bye."

Alan sorely missed his dad and mom since they'd moved south after retirement. He couldn't wait to see them.

But first things first.

Hanging up, he took two gift-wrapped shoe boxes off the counter and ran out of the kitchen.

He wound his way through the crowd of guests, quickly shaking hands and greeting people.

Standing in the front foyer, talking with Sarah, was a friendly-looking couple. Alan recognized Jim Shepherd, his new employee.

"Jim!" Alan called out. "Glad you made it."

"Thanks," Jim replied. "This is my wife, Martha."

"Pleased to meet you," Mrs. Shepherd said, stepping forward to shake Alan's hand.

Mr. Shepherd looked around. "Hmmm, where are the kids?"

But Alan already knew. His eyes had caught them right away. They were making their way to him through the crowd.

"Here they are," Alan said, looking with amazement into two faces he hadn't seen in years.

The faces of Judy and Peter Shepherd.

Mrs. Shepherd gave Alan a puzzled look. "How did you know?"

"Just a guess," Sarah cut in.

Alan took off his Santa beard. He smiled at

Judy and Peter, showing them his real face, half-expecting them to ask about the game. Half-wanting them to. To pick up their old friendship where they'd left off.

"Well, you're right," Mr. Shepherd said. "These are our children, Judy and Peter. Kids, meet Mr. and Mrs. Parrish."

"Hi," Peter mumbled.

"Nice to meet you," Judy added politely.

They don't remember, Alan realized. *They don't remember because it never happened.*

He cast a glance at Sarah. Sadness and joy and relief and awe were all washing across her face. Only Alan could see it.

Because only Alan felt the same things.

"We . . . feel like we already know you," Sarah said softly to the kids.

"We've heard so much about you," Alan quickly offered. He held out the two presents. "Merry Christmas."

As Judy and Peter unwrapped the boxes, Alan snapped back to reality. "So," he said to Mr. Shepherd, "when can you start?"

"Well, actually," Mr. Shepherd replied, "Martha and I were thinking about taking a little skiing trip up in the Canadian Rockies. You know, kind of a second honeymoo — "

"*NO!*" Alan and Sarah both shouted.

The accident had happened on that trip — the accident that had turned Judy and Peter into orphans. Neither Sarah nor Alan could ever forget that.

The Shepherds looked startled by the outburst.

"Sorry," Alan said, "uh, it's just that we — "

"Really need to get the campaign for the new line going," Sarah finished.

"No problem," Mr. Shepherd said a little tentatively. "I can start next week."

Judy and Peter were now holding up their presents — Parrish Shoes' latest line of air-cushioned sneakers, complete with a jungle motif.

Judy read the logo. " 'Ju . . . man . . . ji's'?"

"What do you think?" Alan asked.

"That's a weird name for a sneaker," Peter said.

Pow. Alan felt that one right in the heart. For the first time, he really knew — knew in the deepest part of him — that Jumanji was over.

He didn't miss it a bit.

"Come on," Alan offered, "let me introduce you to everyone."

As he led them into the living room, Mrs.

Shepherd gazed around with admiration. "This is such a wonderful house!"

"Yeah," Mr. Shepherd said with a laugh. "Wouldn't Nora love to get her hands on a place like this. . . ."

PART SIX

SOMEWHERE IN THE SOUTH OF FRANCE, TODAY

CHAPTER 32

Emilie Reynaud and Isabel Villeneuve stroll grimly along the beach, huddling against the chill wind. At twelve years old, they are best friends, united in many things: Their taste in clothing and music, their hatred of school, and their overall misery about life in general. . . .

They are speaking to each other rapidly in their native French.

"My mom and dad are always criticizing me," says Emilie bitterly. "They never let me have any fun."

"It's the same way at my house," Isabel agrees. "Nobody appreciates me!"

The waves lap close to them, just touching their feet. A few meters ahead, something dark and rectangular is jutting out of the sand. Something that has washed up from the sea.

The girls stop talking. Finally, something interesting in their boring lives. They veer over toward it.

And a low drumming sound begins. . . .